# ABOUT THE AUTHOR

Gunvor Johansson was born and grew up in the North of Sweden, where the winters are dark and full of snow and where you will find spectacular displays of Northern Lights. In contrast the summers have the Midnight Sun; a sun which never sets. She came to England as a teenager and has lived there ever since. She now lives on the South Coast. 'The Water People's Secret' is her first Children's book. The second, 'Alice and Friends in her Secret World' is a sequel. She feels strongly about saving the oceans from pollution and destruction and this is reflected in these two books. At the present time she is writing a series of books about a small Troll, who came from Scandinavia but is now living in Scotland.

To Mia,

Enjoy!

# The
# Water People's
# Secret

## Gunvor Johansson

*Gunvor Johansson*

BriarField
PRESS

ISBN 978-1494935573

Book design by The Art of Communication, www.artofcomms.co.uk
Cover image adapted from an original phtograph by Sergii Votit

# Dedication

To my grandchildren Alice and Joseph,

whose names I have used in this book.

# Acknowledgements

My thanks to Hilary and Lorna,
for their constant, friendly help and support
during the writing of this book.

Also my thanks to my friends at Fareham Writer's Group
for their helpful comments.

Chapter 1

# Meeting Zina

Alice stumbled and fell onto the wet pebbles. Her long hair cascaded over her face and she flicked it back, as she got up. She rubbed her grazed knee but didn't give it much thought. Now only a narrow footpath separated her new home from the beach and this was where she'd always wanted to live. The sea intrigued her and she moved closer to the water's edge, drawn to it.

Heavy clouds made the afternoon dark. White horses rode the waves as they crashed onto the beach, making the pebbles rock. She picked up a shell but threw it away when she saw it was broken, a few others she put in her pocket. In front of her the seaweed lashed against the shore only to whirl out again with the next wave. It stinks, she thought and sniffed the air, it smells of medicine.

'Help me, help me!'

She spun around. There was no one, but she'd heard a voice.

'Help me, get me out of here!'

There was no mistake. A tiny voice, clear like a silver bell. But where? After a moment's hesitation she called out, 'Where are you?'

'Over here in the shell,' came the answer.

Alice took several steps backwards, but stopped. What is it? I won't find out by running away, she thought. Moving one foot forward then the other, she stared in the direction of where she'd heard the voice.

'Are you going to help me or not?' the voice sang out.

Taking a deep breath she got down on her knees and crawled. Her sore knee was hurting on the stones, but she didn't care. She turned over a few pebbles and lifted a larger one. Then she saw it! An oyster shell, whose grey colour and shape blended in with the pebbles hiding it. It was the biggest she'd ever seen, and the voice came from a small open slit. With her heart pounding, she put out her hand but quickly pulled it back. Should she pick it up?

'What are you waiting for?'

'Wow! I'm dreaming!'

'No, you're not. Hurry up!'

At last Alice responded, 'Do you bite?' she croaked.

'Don't be silly!'

Cautiously she picked up the shell, trying hard to stop her hand from trembling.

'Get me out and be quick about it!'

She almost dropped the shell.

'Ouch, that hurt. Be careful and let me out.'

'Course I will. But there's such a word as "please," and don't call me silly,' Alice blurted out.

'Oh… all right. Please, please let me out!' The voice wasn't quite so cocky anymore.

'That's better,' Alice muttered.

With her hand still shaking she carefully put down the shell, searching around for something to open it with. She remembered; in her pocket was the key to her diary; she would use that. She inserted the key in the gap between the two halves and wedged it open.

'Wow!' There was a creature in the shell. A tiny girl! She was wearing a tight green shimmering suit made of scales the colour of emeralds, and her long hair shone like copper. Alice leaned closer and could see that it wasn't a suit at all, but part of the girl, the scales covered most of her body and up her neck in a spiky pattern. The scales also went to the sides of her cheeks and in a thin line above her eyes where they ended, giving the impression of eyebrows. In a few places between the scales her darker green skin shone through. It looked silky and smooth like the skin of a seal, and she had webbed fingers and feet. By her side was a gleaming white pearl.

Catching her breath Alice sat down with a thump and a deep sigh, 'Oh, you're pretty. Pretty in a funny way, but not very polite. What are you? Are you real?'

'I'm here, aren't I,' the girl snapped, 'and about time. I've been here for ages. I swam in to collect the pearl and this stupid shell slammed shut. Then the waves washed it onto the beach, I thought I'd never get out.'

Alice's cheeks burned. 'Who do you think you are? And whatever you are, you don't seem very grateful. If you don't mind me saying so, I think you're rude.'

'Never mind what you think, my father is worried about me. I was nearly carried away by a dog, but thank goodness he only had a good sniff. That scared me! No wonder I'm impatient. Believe me, I'm so glad you came along.' The sullenness disappeared and the girl's face lit up in a big friendly smile.

Alice couldn't help but smile back. I can't be cross, she thought. She could see warmth and laughter in the green eyes shining back at her.

'I've been waiting for you!' the girl said.

'Have you?'

'Yes, I've heard grown-ups but I can't call out to them.'

'Why?'

'They don't belong in our world.'

'Oh, I see,' Alice said. 'What's your world and who are you?'

'My name is Zina. I'm a princess of the Water People.'

'Of the what?' Alice's eyes widened.

'The Water People! My father is the king. I come from another world that exists under the sea. Your people don't know we are there. Everything is much smaller, like I am.'

'I don't believe you!'

'It's true. We are the Water People. Our world is hidden within your sea, we've been there for ages. But now I must return, I've heard my people calling for me through the waves. Will you help me back into the sea?'

'Of course I will, but stay a bit longer! This is exciting. I want to talk to you. My name is Alice, but my friends call me Ally. Today we moved into the house over there. I have a brother, Joseph. He is three years above me at school, and my mum and dad are Maggie and William.' She took a deep breath. 'What are your parents called?'

Zina laughed, 'That's a lot of information. My father is King Merl and my mother Queen Sira. And I've also got magic powers. Listen to what I say! You must never repeat it to anyone, not even your parents. You're the only human I can tell, because you're special.'

'Really?' Alice blinked.

'Yes, I can feel it.'

'Yes! I feel different now that I've met you. Can I tell Joseph, my brother?'

'No, he is human.'

'Joseph? I suppose he is … sometimes.'

'As a thank you for saving me, I'll give you this pearl. I've made it magic, it will grant you five wishes. You can save them for as long as you like but when they are gone they are gone, so choose them wisely. As soon as you say "I wish…" it will happen.'

Alice's eyes lit up with excitement, 'Wow! Cool!'

'But take care! There are rules to remember. The moon must be full between each wish. Do you understand what that means?' Zina stared hard at her.

Alice frowned, 'I think so. The moon is full once a month. That means I can only have one wish in the same month.'

Zina nodded, 'That's right. Never tell anyone about the pearl and me. If you do, it will lose its power. Take good care of it.'

'Can I have a wish now?'

'Yes. What's your wish?'

Alice closed her eyes, but quickly flicked them open and blurted out, 'I wish that we can be friends and I want to meet you again.'

'You'll have your wish.' Zina eye's twinkled, 'I too want to see you again. I'll meet you here but only after the full moon has passed three times.'

'Why do I have to wait? I want to ask you lots of things.'

'I have a reason. If you don't tell anyone, then I'll know I can trust you. Now I must leave. Take the pearl and don't lose it, and please, put me back into the sea.'

Alice waded into the freezing water until her ankles were submerged and gently lowered the shell into the sea. With a flip of her webbed feet and a wave Zina swam away. Would she see her again? 'Bye, Zina, bye.'

Chapter 2

# Keeping a Secret

I'd better hurry, Alice thought, as she ran home, Mum will be missing me. It will be hard to keep this a secret. I'm bursting to tell someone, but it will be worth it when I see the Water Girl again. All these thoughts whirled around in her head.

She opened the garden gate and hurried across the lawn to her new home. It was a white-washed two storey cottage with a black roof and black window frames. She knew she'd be happy here. She went in through the veranda doors and saw that her father and Joseph had arrived. Both had stayed behind to lock up their old house. Joseph stuck out his tongue, as he walked past carrying a cardboard box. Alice grimaced back.

Her mother was kneeling by a large chest, a stack of china plates stood on the floor beside her. Pushing back an unruly curl of her short brown hair, she flashed her violet eyes at her daughter, 'Alice, where have you been? There's so much to do, I need your help.'

'Sorry, Mum,' Alice mumbled

'Look at you! Your trainers and jeans are soaked. Go and get changed or you'll catch a cold. Your clothes are in the case on the floor. Unpack it. Then come down and make us a cup of tea.'

'OK. I'm sorry, Mum, I forgot the time. I was looking for shells.'

She ran upstairs. Waiting outside the door was her cat. Picking him up she stroked his fluffy orange coat. 'Do you like your new home? Great, isn't it? Oh, Simba, you're heavy, you should lose weight.' She dropped him onto the floor, Simba followed her in.

It will only take five minutes to unpack this, she thought, and turned the case upside down on the bed. A photo tumbled out, taken on a recent skiing trip to Sweden. It was special to her. She'd framed the photo herself, and packed it carefully amongst her clothes. It had been such a happy holiday. The family stood on a veranda, outside a ski-lodge, where they had just finished drinking hot chocolate. She and Joseph stood either side of their parents;

all were dressed in colourful ski gear, snow-goggles lying on the table beside them. In the picture you could see mountains, lots of snow and a blue sky. It had been warm enough in the sun to remove their hats and gloves. Joseph was thin and nearly as tall as his mother and had her curly hair; otherwise he looked much like his dad with his pale blue eyes. Alice knew that her mum looked younger than her forty years, everyone said so. She put the photo on the window sill and rushed downstairs to make the tea. Her clothes left forgotten in a heap on the bed.

\*

Before Alice climbed into bed, she sat down in front of Simba's basket. She had got permission for Simba to sleep in her bedroom, but only for that very first night. 'Sit up!'

Simba yawned.

'It's important. Something I can't tell any human being. No one on earth. Since you're a cat, I can. Today I met a princess, her name is Zina.' As she continued her story Simba's green eyes didn't flicker once. 'You believe me, don't you? Look, here is the pearl.' Simba's eyes got wider as he looked at the pearl, but still she couldn't be sure that he understood the importance of her story. 'When the full moon has passed three times I can meet her again. I must find a calendar to see when that is. I hope it will go quickly. What do you think? Will she come?' Simba squinted back at her but there was no way of telling what his thoughts were.

Chapter 3

# Waiting for the Moon

'How time flies.' Alice's mother hung the calendar back onto the kitchen wall, 'Soon we'll have been here for three months. Where has it gone?' Alice looked up from her maths book. She'd studied the calendar and the cycle of the moon carefully, counting the days.

'Mum, it has dragged!' she protested.

'Alice, you can't be serious. It has flown by!'

'Not to me it hasn't.'

Mum doesn't know, she thought, seven more days and it would be another full moon; the third since she'd found Princess Zina. Her stomach fluttered. Seven days, seven days, she repeated. If it hadn't been for the pearl, she might have thought she'd imagined it all. Sometimes she hid it at the back of her wardrobe, in a little box wrapped in cotton wool, but mostly she kept it in her pocket.

But her world shattered when her mother said, 'We're going to Granny's this week-end. We haven't seen her since Easter.'

'Mum, must we go? I want to stay here.'

'Why? You like visiting Granny.'

'Yes, but not this Saturday. Can't we go next week-end? School will be finished then.'

'Granny will be away. She's off to a climate change conference.'

Alice choked and ran out of the kitchen with tears blurring her eyes. In her room she took out the pearl. 'I've waited for so long to see Zina and now I won't be able to,' a tear fell onto the pearl and she wiped it off with her sleeve. She sobbed herself to sleep that night.

*

At school she had made several friends but spent most of her time with Lizzy, who was kind and a good friend.

During the break Lizzy put an arm around her shoulder, 'What's the matter, Ally?'

'Nothing.' Alice looked away.

'You look sad. You can tell me.' Lizzy's eyes were full of concern.

'I can't. I've promised a friend.'

'Who's that? What's she like?' Lizzy asked.

Alice hesitated, 'Like you, she's really nice. She's got red hair as well, but she hasn't got your freckles. Sorry, can't tell you more.'

Lizzy yanked her arm away, 'All right, but I thought I was your best friend.'

'You are my best friend. Honestly! Don't be cross. Please, let us be friends again?' Alice's eyes started to burn.

'Sure.' Lizzy nodded and hugged her, 'Sorry, I didn't mean to upset you even more.'

*

As Alice walked into the kitchen after school, her mother said, 'You'll be getting your way after all. Gran phoned and told me that she had a dream about the sea. She woke up with the notion to come here instead, she's missing the fresh air. Remember I told you that Granny used to live not far from here, when she was a girl. Anyway it's settled and she'll stay for a few days, before she's off to her conference.'

Alice ran to her room and took out the pearl from its hiding place, 'I knew it! Zina promised me my wish, and I will have it.' She kissed the pearl, she was happy.

## Chapter 4

# Plastic Porridge

'I thought I'd take the train instead of driving. A small contribution to saving the planet,' Granny said, when Alice and her mother met her at the station. As Granny got off the train, Alice's mum stepped back to look her up and down.

'Mother, I like what you've done to your hair. It's nice.'

Granny adjusted her glasses before she answered, 'Thanks, Maggie. Yes, I've gone ash blonde. I don't want my grey to show yet.' Granny should look ancient, being so old, but she doesn't, thought Alice.

After lunch her mother and Granny settled in the garden to read. Granny waved, 'Come over here,

Alice, I want to show you my book about marine conservation.' Alice stared with open mouth at the picture of a beach in Hawaii; covered with plastic of all kind.

Granny nodded when she saw her expression, 'Yes, it's hard to believe. There's an area in the Pacific Ocean, where the plastic debris goes down to a depth of ten metres. That's more than the height of your house!'

'You're joking, Granny?'

'No, I wish I was. The sea currents carry it there. The scary thing is that we can't get rid of it. It will be there for many hundreds of years.'

'That's wicked!'

'Yes, it is, and it is killing birds and other sea animals in their thousands.'

Alice shuddered, 'It's like plastic porridge! What can we do about it?'

'Not a lot. We can't clean the oceans, they are too big, but we can stop adding to it.'

Alice's mother shook her head, 'If only people would take their rubbish home. It would make such a difference.'

Alice glanced at her watch. Soon it would be three o'clock, the time she'd found the shell and Zina. 'Mum, I'm going to the beach. Is that OK?'

'Just make sure Joseph knows where you are.'

'She'll be all right,' Granny said.

Her mother nodded. 'Joseph is on the beach, he'll keep an eye on her. We went swimming every week in Brinham. The indoor pool was excellent and she's a strong swimmer.'

'Do you regret moving?' Granny asked.

'No, I love living here by the sea. Like you did as a child,' her mother answered.

Alice waved and skipped across the lawn to the garden gate. The sun shone warm on her back. In April, three months ago, it had been cold with nobody on the beach. Today it was full of people, so how could Zina show herself? She stared towards the spot where Zina had swum away. Would she come?

## Chapter 5

# Zina Returns

'Please, please, let her be there,' Alice whispered. Did something move in the water? Yes, a fish. She waded out further and jerked to a halt; something touched her leg. Her heart skipped: it was Zina from under the surface!

She looked around to see if anyone was watching. It was OK, she swam out. Zina came up close and whispered in her ear, 'Would you like to become a Water Girl and come with me to my world?'

'Oh yes! But… but how can I?'

'It's possible!'

'Really! Tell me!'

'Swallow this!' Zina held out what looked like

a miniature blueberry. 'Close your eyes; take a deep breath and let yourself sink.'

'I'm not sure. Will I be safe?'

'Yes, and you won't be away for long.'

Alice carefully took the berry; it was so small, she was afraid she would drop it. Squeezing her eyes shut, she swallowed it, but in the next second her eyes flew open as a strong buzz went through her. It only lasted for a moment.

She inhaled sharply and looked down in wonder at the shimmering blue scales which now covered her. Her arms sparkled as if sprayed with sequins when she moved. Touching her neck with both hands she could feel the scales going up to her chin, just as they did on Zina. Her blue skin, which wasn't covered by scales, felt firm and smooth. She spread out her hands, her fingers were webbed. She bent over to look at her bare feet and could see the web between her toes. This is mad! But exciting, she thought.

'Blue suits your blonde hair and dark eyes.' Zina laughed seeing the expression on Alice's face. 'Do you like it?'

'Yes, oh yes! I can breathe under water and I've shrunk. This is magic!'

The pebbles scattered on the seabed were the size of small boulders. The kelp, now tall as trees, swayed gently, their fronds pointing towards the surface. They reminded her of palm trees with upside-down crowns. On some of them, she saw huge sea urchins climbing up the stems to graze on the fronds. At that moment the water became choppy and the kelp lurched as if hit by a hurricane. The girls heard a tremendous noise and a dark shadow passed overhead.

Alice toppled over and splashed about frantically to regain her balance. The colour drained from her face, 'What's happening?'

'It's a motorboat. You should hear the big ones.'

What had she done? Would she be safe? She brushed away the thoughts and gave Zina a weak smile.

Zina took hold of her hand to reassure her, 'You're like me now, you'll be all right.'

Alice was surprised at how cold Zina's hand was, but gave it a squeeze and managed another smile, 'Why is your hand so cold, Zina?'

'Well, we are part fish. You too now! Feel yours!'

Alice rubbed her hands together, 'Oh yes, so they are. Weird!'

'But come on, Father wants to thank you for saving me. We're going to the kingdom of the Water People. Follow closely behind!'

Alice made her feet move in unison to act like flippers but for the second time she ended up thrashing about with flailing arms. 'Wait! Stop! I'm sinking.'

Zina swam back to her. 'You're not doing it right. Look at me. Gently move up and down like this. See?'

She stretched out her legs and moved as Zina showed her, but only sank further ending up on the seabed. 'Let's try again. Push yourself off and wriggle,' Zina said.

'I'm doing my best.' Alice pinched her lips together.

'We'll try something else,' Zina said patiently. 'Hold my hand and we'll swim side by side until you've got the hang of it. I won't go fast.'

'Can't you use magic to make me swim?'

'No, I can't. Some things you'll have to learn for yourself. Come on now.'

Alice gritted her teeth and made up her mind, she was going to manage this. It worked. Soon she kept up with Zina.

'That's better, I can let go of your hand. Follow me.'

A distance away Alice saw a stream of cloudy water. 'What is it?'

'Oh that! It's man-made. Stuff your people pollute the sea with,' Zina answered grim faced. 'The girls hurriedly swam past.

When they arrived by a tall forest of kelp, Zina searched for the hidden opening in the dense grass-wall. Finding it, she held out a helping hand to Alice,

'We call this the Forest Gate. Come on! We'll push through here. We are in my world now.'

Alice nodded in reply, too stunned to speak. Amazing! On the other side of the wall inside the forest, everything was in comparison the right size. For a while they swam amongst a swaying meadow of brown and red seaweed, some of which was slimy to touch. She kept her eyes on Zina, careful to follow within easy reach of her flipper feet.

Alice inhaled sharply; she'd been brought to a halt. Her legs wouldn't move. Glancing over her shoulder; she saw thick strings of black hair winding themselves around her feet pulling her away. The next moment, a strand of hair wound itself around her neck preventing her from calling out. She began to choke and splutter.

## Chapter 6

# An Invisible Enemy

Zina carried on swimming, several lengths ahead, unaware that Alice was in danger. Alice tugged desperately at the hair around her neck and managed to loosen it enough to breathe again.

'Zina!' she shouted. She grabbed hold of the grass to stop herself being dragged further back, but it was slippery and slid through her fingers. 'Help!' she screamed.

Too late! She disappeared into the weedy grass. She flung out her arms setting the seaweed swaying and caught a glimpse of Zina swimming towards her at a furious speed.

'Here! I'm here!'

Zina swam up with a dagger in her mouth. Her eyes glinting like steel. With a swift movement the dagger was in her hand and she cut the strings binding Alice's legs. Quickly and without speaking she yanked off the strand of hair around her neck.

'Stay here!' Zina ordered.

'Don't leave me!' Alice shouted.

Zina just waved and swam into the weed following the trailing black hair. Alice trembled as she removed the loose strands wrapped around her feet. She pressed up against the weed to make herself less visible. Any sudden movement of the seaweed would signal Zina's return, or worse, that of her enemy. The sea around her remained calm, but she couldn't stop shaking. It seemed ages before Zina came back.

'What's happening? You said I'd be safe.'

'Sorry, I didn't expect this.' Zina' eyes flickered and she avoided looking at her. 'We'd better not mention this to father or he might not let you visit again.'

Alice's lips quivered, 'I've only just got here and already I've been attacked. I'm not sure I want to come again.'

'You will! You'll change your mind when you see where I live.' Zina's face lit up, 'Come on, give me your hand, we'll swim side by side.'

Alice searched Zina's eyes, as she hesitantly took

her outstretched hand. Zina was hiding something from her. What was it?

Chapter 7

# A World Full of Colour

Out of the forest they swam in clear water surrounded by fish. Alice could see reefs around them, with yellow coral like miniature trees. Others had the colour of raspberries and she recognized the red fan coral. Bunches of sea cucumbers swayed back and forth and red sponges were floating like balloons. She could see starfish and brilliant sea anemones. The fish dipped their heads in a respectful greeting to Zina. Wow, she really is a princess, Alice thought.

She gaped at what she saw, thin blue fish with yellow stripes and fat yellow fish with blue stripes. A spiky fish came close to her and immediately puffed itself up to double its size. Another huge red fish with black spots brushed up against her. But when she saw two black sinister-looking fish with long hairy moustaches, she moved closer to Zina. 'Bother!' she muttered.

Other plain fish could barely be seen, as they blended in with the background, and looked like streaks of silver as they flashed past. The fish circled around and dashed in and out of giant shells. 'Look!' Alice called out. 'Oh, just look at this! There are sea flowers looking like purple tulips and some like cactus with huge yellow buds.' Above her she saw enormous pink floating water lilies, attached by their stalks to the seabed, forming a ceiling. The fish sheltered underneath their umbrellas.

Wonderful! She couldn't take her eyes off the sight and bumped into Zina, who had stopped in front of a high wall made of seaweed, tightly woven together.

'We've arrived, Ally.'

'You live here?'

'Yes, behind this wall is my father's palace. Earlier, when we swam through the forest of tall sea grass, we entered the land of the Water People. It can only be reached the way we came. The entrance is hidden. You'd never find it on your own. You're honoured to be the first human here. Come on, let's swim over the top. There are stingrays guarding the wall to stop intruders. They won't hurt you.'

But Alice carefully avoided their long needle sharp tails.

The stingrays parted to let them through and they swam over the wall. A ship rested on the seabed, covered in shells and coral. The shells gave off a pale blue light. The water sparkled with colour.

'Oh, this is cool!'

'Yes, there's no pollution in our world, unlike yours, so everything here is healthy. Father decided to make this ship his palace. We've done a lot of work to it, as you can see.'

Water People swam by staring curiously at her. Alice waved and was greeted with smiles. Although I'm a stranger they seem friendly enough, she thought.

She followed Zina into the ship and they came to a large room. 'This is where Father makes his decisions and where we have our celebrations,' Zina said. A broad shouldered Water Man was sitting on a giant shell, at the back of the room. His silvery scales were sending bright flashes in all directions, but the scales going up the side of his face and forming his eyebrows were black. He looked stern, forbidding even. He sat upright, his white hair flowing down to his shoulders. But, as Alice swam closer she could see that he wasn't an old man and his eyes were kind.

'Father, this is Ally.'

The king studied her for a moment before he

spoke, 'My name is King Merl. I'll always be grateful to you for saving my daughter.' He was interrupted by a Water Man swimming towards them.

'Your Majesty, I've an urgent message for you.' He handed a shell to the king who held it to his ear, and listened with furrowed eyebrows.

'Do you have mobiles here?' Alice asked.

'Mobiles? You mean the phones people carry about,' Zina answered. 'No, we don't need phones; the water carries our messages. We've different frequencies, but they can be listened in to. We use shells, when there is a need for secrecy. You can only hear by holding it to your ear.'

The king spoke into the shell, 'Here, take my answer back.' The wrinkles on his forehead disappeared when he turned to the girls, 'I'm sorry but I must leave you, a matter of urgency. Zina, make your friend welcome and show her our palace and the gardens. I hope to see you again, Ally. Goodbye for now.'

'Oh, can I? Can I really come again?' She had already forgotten the attack in the forest.

'Let's hope so,' the king nodded.

She followed Zina through the many rooms. Everyone living in the palace had his or her own little chamber. The rooms were sparsely decorated, although most walls had a covering of pearl, which made it very bright. Attractive seaweed grew in the corners and some particularly beautiful corals decorated the walls.

'Come on, now for the gardens. We grow almost everything we eat. Look at these; they are sea plums, very tasty.' Zina held out a mauve coloured fruit, 'Try it!'

Alice hesitated, before she bit into it, 'Yuk.' She spat it out, 'It's fishy.'

'It's delicious.' Zina took another bite of hers.

'Hmm, I think we've different taste in food,' laughed Alice, 'but what's that funny looking fruit?'

'That's the Royal Pear, named after Father. He found it and we've managed to grow many more. Like to try one?'

'No thanks.'

'Well, then follow me.' Zina disappeared into a large shell.

'It's dark in here. I can't see you, Zina.'

'It has to be, this is where we breed snails. They like it dark. Your eyes will adjust.'

Zina was right. Soon she could see row upon row of large fronds with curled up edges all filled with snails. 'You must eat loads.'

'Mmm, we do.' Zina held out a snail for Alice who shook her head; so she popped it into her own mouth.

Alice's eyes widened, 'You eat them raw?'

'Of course! That's our way.'

'I thought you might use magic.'

'Magic is only used at special times. Here comes Loya, he's the keeper of the snails.'

A Water Man appeared out of the darkness. He had a grey, short beard and deep furrows in his cheeks. He swam in a slow motion; moving steadily forward. He eyed Alice with suspicion.

'Loya, this is Ally. She's my friend; she's here on a visit. It's all right, we can trust her.' Loya nodded but didn't speak.

Once outside Zina said, 'Don't worry about him, he's old and mistrusts anything new. I think he's spent too long in the darkness. Most of us Water People are very friendly, as you'll see.'

'He's the oldest one of your people I've seen. How old is he? His scales look brittle and faded.'

'I don't know. We don't do age. You'd hardly notice us getting old. We haven't got hours and days like you do. But he's been around a long time.'

'Has he spent all the time inside that shell?'

'No, only since he retired from his duty as one of my father's guards,' Zina laughed.

'Can I meet your mother?'

Zina turned away sharply and Alice thought that she wouldn't answer. 'No, my mother isn't here, perhaps some other time.' Zina still wouldn't look at her. She's very upset, Alice thought. I wonder why?

Chapter 8

# The Land Adventure Expedition

Alice wanted to ask Zina why she was upset, but forgot when four girls swam up to them. They didn't keep still but moved about in a dancing motion. Their scales were all in different colours and it made the water shimmer.

'Zina, can we meet your friend? Please, can I touch you?' A pretty Water Girl, with green hair, didn't wait for an answer but ran her hands through Alice's blond hair, which flowed above her head. 'Gold,' she said, 'that makes you different from us.

No one here has that colour.' Ana bowed to her.

Zina pointed at the girls. 'This is Ana you've just met and Nor her sister, and this is Silla and Haja.'

Alice stared at Nor whose body looked as if it was made of ice, her scales were pale, giving out a blue sheen. Nor met her gaze with smiling cool blue eyes, 'You're the first human we've seen, as we haven't been on our Land Adventure Expedition yet.' She did a twirl in front of Alice, laying both hands on her shoulders.

Alice jumped at the touch and blushed, 'Sorry, your hands are so cold. But what's the Land Adventure Expedition?'

Nor stopped dancing and put a hand in front of her mouth. 'Oops, I shouldn't have said.'

Zina frowned, 'Can't tell you, Ally. I must ask permission from Father first.'

'How come you know so much about our life on land?'

'That's part of it, but I've already said too much. I must take you back to your world.'

'Sorry, I've asked too many questions.' Alice bit her lip.

'Oh no, that's not the reason. It's time for you to go back, that's all.'

Alice waved to the girls and followed Zina. Up and up they swam until they reached the top of the palace wall and again the stingrays parted to let them through. From up there they dived down amongst the colourful fish, sending them scattering in all directions. Except one. The menacing black fish with the long moustache trailing either side of his mouth, came so close that the hairs floated across Alice's feet. She shuddered, it reminded her of the hairy black strings that had ensnared her in the forest.

Zina stared hard at the fish and put her hand out to Alice, 'Stay close to me. He can't be trusted.'

'Did that fish attack me?' Alice asked.

'No, not him.' Zina snapped, her lips pressed together.

Better not to ask any more questions, Alice thought, sneaking a sideways glance at her friend's stony face. She kept her mouth shut as they swam through the forest. At the place called the Forest Gate, where the kelp was closely packed together, Zina stopped, 'We'll push through here. On the other side we're back in your sea.'

As they made their way through the tough sea grasses into Alice's world, she was immediately struck by the much stronger movement of the water and the enormous size of everything surrounding them. A seahorse, as big as herself, gently floated past. Weird, she thought.

Zina pointed, 'Over there is your beach. I have to go back now.' She held out a tiny berry, 'Take this.'

'Wait! When can I see you again?'

'I don't know, I'll come and find you.' With a splash she was gone.

'See you!' Alice called out after her.

As soon as she'd swallowed the berry, she felt the strong tingling sensation. She became human again. There was no sign of her scaly body. Spreading out her fingers she examined them closely. She lifted up her foot; the web between her toes was gone. 'Did I dream this?' She swam ashore and sat down on the beach.

She saw Joseph approaching on his windsurfer, he waded in pulling it behind him, 'There you are, Ally. Where have you been?'

'Oh, here and there swimming about. What time is it?'

'Quarter past three,' Joseph answered.

Surely she'd been away for more than fifteen minutes? But Zina had said there was no such thing as time in her world. 'Can't be! Are you sure that's the right time?'

'Yeah, it is. Will you keep an eye on the board for me, Sis? You can have a go if you like.'

'No thanks, but I'll look after it.'

Joseph returned twenty minutes later and set off surfing again. But she stayed for a time staring out to sea, listening to the soothing lapping of the waves. It had been a magic day, but, she chewed her lips, there had also been danger. She needed time to think and to understand what had happened to her. And she wanted to know more about the Land Adventure Expedition. What ever could it mean? But Zina had been very secretive. She desperately wanted to share this with someone. It was too big a secret to keep. But the magic would disappear if she did. Wouldn't it? Would she dare to tell?

Chapter 9

# Alice Makes a Wish

'What's the hurry? Got someone chasing you?' Her father looked up from his newspaper as Alice came rushing into the kitchen.

'Some good-looking boy you met on the beach or a sea monster perhaps?' Granny winked.

'Why would anyone want to chase after Alice?' her mother teased.

'Oh, I can see lots of reasons. The dimples on her cheeks, and those dark violet eyes, Maggie, like yours,' Granny said.

'Don't get a big head, Alice,' her mother laughed. 'You'd better wash before dinner. I expect you're full of sand.' Her mother peered into the oven, 'The baked potatoes won't be long.'

In her bedroom Alice ran over to the freestanding, full-length mirror and adjusted it so that she could see herself from head to toe. She tried to imagine the sparkling blue fish-scales covering her body. She ran her fingers up the side of her face, and over her eyebrows to where the scales would've ended. If only she could see herself as one of the Water People. What she saw was a young girl, neither fat nor thin and tall for her age, which pleased her as it made her look older. Lifting up her head, she fingered a tiny scar under her chin. It had faded and didn't show much. She'd got it by falling out of a plum tree when she was six years old.

She sighed and turned to Simba, who was fast asleep on her bed. 'So you've sneaked up.' Bending down she kissed the back of his head. 'You won't believe what I've done! I've been a Water Girl with scales on my body and web between my fingers and toes! I've been to Princess Zina's world.'

Simba, who wasn't quite awake, stood up unsteadily. 'I'll tell you all about it later. I've got to go down to dinner now.' Alice kissed the top of his head again.

Downstairs they were ready to eat. 'Where is Joseph? I hope nothing has happened to him,' Granny said.

'He's a sensible boy but he must learn to keep

time, especially when you're here, Maud.' Alice could tell by her father's frown that he was annoyed.

At that moment the door was flung open and Joseph hobbled in, supported by his best friend Tom.

'I'm OK,' Joseph said, although he was grimacing, 'just a twisted ankle. I collided with another surfer. Can you take a look, Dad?'

'Good job it wasn't a boat,' Tom said, helping Joseph to sit down on the nearest chair. Tom brushed back his shoulder length blond hair and smiled.

His hair is too long, but he's nice, I like him, Alice thought.

Joseph's father examined the ankle. 'It's all right, Son, nothing broken, just a sprain.'

'Oh, what a relief! It's handy to have a doctor in the house.' Granny patted her son-in-law on the back.

Alice watched as everyone fussed over Joseph. He could've had a horrible accident. It made her feel bad to think about it. At once she knew; for her second wish, she would ask for Joseph to be safe on his windsurfer. He doesn't mean to be nasty when he teases me, brothers behave like that at times, she thought.

After dinner she hurried upstairs. Simba was asleep, curled up just inside the door. Alice tripped and jumped over him, 'Simba, do you have to lie in the middle of the floor?'

She stopped and stared; the little box that had contained the pearl was on the floor, the lid lying next to it. The cotton wool, which it had been wrapped in, was shredded into little pieces scattered over the carpet.

The pearl was nowhere to be seen.

'My pearl,' she shrieked, 'where is it?' She stamped her foot.

Simba opened one eye and yawned.

'Where is it? What have you done with it?' She sank down onto her knees and examined the pieces of cotton wool, the pearl wasn't amongst them. Simba yawned again.

'You horrid cat, don't go to sleep, I want my pearl.'

Simba sat up, his green eyes looking back at her.

'This pearl is important!'

She crawled around the floor, wiping away tears with the back of her hand. She wriggled under the bed, looked under the desk and sent her shoes, bags and an assortment of magazines flying out from the bottom of the wardrobe.

No pearl.

It had to be somewhere. All at once she knew where it could be: in Simba's stomach! That cat would eat anything, no wonder he was fat.

'Oh, how I wish you could talk. Simba, you have swallowed it. I know you have.'

'No, I haven't.'

Alice's face paled; her mouth fell open, but no sound came. Her legs gave way from under her and she slid to the floor. She stammered, 'Sim-Sim, was-was that you talk-talking?'

'Yep, it was me. Guess you got your wish. That's what you asked for just now. Remember?' Simba said with a lazy drawl.

Alice gaped at him, not believing, 'I did! I wished you could talk, and now you can. I don't need to hold the pearl; I don't even know where it is.'

'I do.'

'Tell me, quickly, tell me!'

'Hmm yes, but promise to ask your mum not to give me the cat food with lamb flavour. You know how fond I was of our neighbour's pet lamb in Brinham. We used to play together.'

'I remember. How sweet of you, Simba. I promise.'

'Another thing; ask your dad to check that I'm in before he locks the cat flap. Sometimes I've to stay out in all weather.'

'I will. If only you'd wear a collar with a magnet, and you could let your self in. Now where is the pearl?'

'Under the bed.'

'No, it's not, I've looked there.'

'Yes, it is. It's stuck in a gap between the floor

and the skirting board. I tried to get it out but my claw kept on catching.'

'Show me!' Simba held up his paw. 'No, not your claw, silly! Show me where the pearl is.'

They both crawled under the bed. 'There.' Simba pointed.

'I can see it! I need something thin to poke it out with.' Alice wriggled out.

At that moment her mother came into the room. 'What on earth are you doing and who are you talking to?'

'Simba, he's under the bed.'

'You know I don't want him in your room.'

'Please, please can he stay a bit longer? It's important! I'll bring him down soon.'

'Why is it important?'

'Oh, it just is, Mum, please!'

'I give up with you. Only five minutes then. Now where's your washing?' Her mother picked up some clothes which had dropped onto the floor.

As soon as her mother left the room, Alice grabbed a penknife from her desk drawer and crawled back under the bed. 'This is exciting, Simba. It's like having a new friend. You've always been my friend of course. But now that you can talk, I'm over the moon.' She pushed the knife into the gap and carefully eased out the pearl.

'It looks fine, no harm done. You must promise

me never to play with it again.'

'OK. It wasn't much fun anyway, it was boring.'

'But now I'll have to wait for the next full moon before I can have another wish. I was going to ask the pearl to keep Joseph safe. But I guess he'll just have to be more careful.'

'Tell me what happened today? Can't believe you've been to Zina's world! Just thinking of water scares me.' Simba shook himself.

Alice told him about her transformation into a Water Girl and of her wonderful visit to the Water People's world. Simba didn't have the usual "I couldn't care less look," but listened with his ears pricked up. 'Could be dangerous, Ally, but it sure is an adventure. Beats having all the cream in your mum's fridge.'

'Is food all you think about?'

Simba closed his eyes for a second and shook his head.

'Why are you shaking your head? You can still talk, can't you?' Alice's voice trembled.

Simba nodded.

'Oh, there you go again. Speak to me!' Simba squinted back at her, his eyes two narrow slits, but he said nothing. 'Please, talk to me!'

Simba only stared, this time he didn't even nod or shake his head. 'I knew it was too good to last. I so need you to talk to and now you can't.' Alice said with tears running down her cheeks.

'I didn't mean to upset you,' Simba spoke again.

'You horrid cat, you're as bad as Joseph, teasing me all the time. Thank goodness you can still talk.' She picked him up and cuddled him.

'Steady on! I only wanted to find out what it was like not to talk again, that's all.' Simba drawled whilst purring loudly.

'You'd better go downstairs. I know I told Mum I was speaking to you, but she doesn't know that you can answer. Don't talk to anyone else. I hate to think what would happen if you do. Just imagine it!'

Chapter 10

# The Water People's Secret

On Friday the last day of term, Alice threw her school bag on the floor and changed into her swimming costume, as soon as she got home.

'Wait a minute,' her mother called out as she ran through the kitchen. 'Where are you off to?'

'I'm going to the beach to meet a friend,' Alice answered.

'You've been rushing off every single afternoon this week.'

'I know. My friend hasn't turned up yet, but she'll come. I know she will, and I want to see her.'

'All right but don't be late for dinner, like

yesterday.'

'I won't, Mum.'

*

Once in the water she swam around and waited for
Zina. When she got tired she floated on her back,
gently moving her arms to keep her balance.

'What are you up to? You've been in the same
spot for the past twenty minutes.' It was Joseph
calling out to her.

'I saw a pretty shell, but I can't find it,' Alice
answered.

'I'll help; I'm pretty good at holding my breath.'

'No thanks, I can manage.'

'I will, that's what brothers are for. It will be my
good deed for the day.'

'I wish you wouldn't.' But Joseph disappeared
beneath the surface. I don't want him here. Zina
won't show herself. Guess it's my own fault for
telling a fib, she thought.

It seemed ages before Joseph showed his head,
taking two deep breaths and disappearing again.
Why did he have to be so helpful today?

Joseph surfaced. 'Sorry, can't see any shell, Sis.'

'It's OK. Really it is. You can go now.' She
watched as Joseph swam ashore and wandered off.

There! A flash of green. She dived.

Zina swum onto her shoulder, grabbing hold of
Alice's hair to steady herself, she spoke directly into

her ear, 'Do you want to come with me?'

Alice nodded and reached for the berry in Zina's hand. 'Wow!' Alice flung out her arms as once again she was transformed into a Water Girl, covered with the shimmering blue scales. 'Whoopee!' She ran her hands over her arms feeling the scales. She spread out her webbed fingers and then bent down to touch the web between her toes. Zina watched with a broad smile.

Alice turned to her, 'I thought you were never coming.'

'I had to hang around. I thought that boy was never leaving. Why did he call you Sis?'

'That's Joseph, my brother. Sis is short for sister, you see.'

'He's good-looking.'

'Joseph! Good-looking? My goodness!' Alice screeched with laughter and did a somersault.

'I think so and he looks strong, but he isn't like you. Your brother has brown hair and his eyes are pale blue, not dark like yours.'

'Yes, he looks like Dad.'

'I see. Now follow me.' Zina swam away.

'Wait, wait, I'll need to get the hang of this.' Alice splashed with her arms and kicked with her legs, to regain her balance. It worked and she swam at a good speed.

'We'll soon be in the forest.' Zina called out.

Remembering her last visit, she stayed close to her friend and repeatedly glanced behind her. She sensed that they were not alone, and as she got used to the gloom, she caught glimpses of eyes following them. Twisting and turning amongst the sea grass she trembled as she brushed up against it, afraid of what was hiding inside.

Leaving the forest she grabbed hold of Zina's arm, 'I was scared, I could see eyes following us.'

'I know. We are being spied on. Soon I'll be able to tell you what's happening.'

'I wonder what Mum would say if she knew about this,' Alice muttered.

'What's that?' Zina raised her eyebrows.

'Nothing! Just thinking out loud.'

Arriving in the clearing, in front of the palace, the huge wall of seaweed loomed ahead of them. Several of the colourful fish swam up to take a closer look.

'They are as curious about you as you are about them,' Zina said, 'but hurry, Father is waiting.'

Alice's mouth fell open when she saw, not the stingrays but a huge number of jellyfish guarding the top of the wall. She recognized them as Portuguese men-of-war, which she had learnt at school. They looked like transparent lumps of blue-white jelly with streamers hanging from their bodies. She shuddered.

'Don't touch their tentacles, they are extremely poisonous. We've been under attack, so they are here to help our soldiers,' Zina explained.

Once inside the palace they swam directly to the big hall. 'Welcome back, Ally.' King Merl gestured to the girls to sit down on two small shells beside him. 'We've decided to tell you everything and with a reason. On your first visit, you asked to meet Zina's mother. Well, she's not here. She's been kidnapped and is held hostage by the people from the Dark Sea.'

Alice's hands shot up to cover her mouth, 'Who are the people from the Dark Sea?'

'Our enemies. They live in a different part of our world, where the water is deep, and where there is no sunlight. We don't often see them and I hope you'll never have to. They reward others to spy and do their dirty work.' The king continued, 'The Dark Sea People want to know how we can go into your world on the Land Adventure Expedition.'

Alice opened her eyes wide and interrupted the king, 'You can come ashore?'

'Yes, we can, but if we tell them how, it will be a threat to your world as well as ours.' The expression on the king's face changed; he looked tired and repeatedly stroked his forehead. 'But unless we do, they won't release Zina's mother. So, we are at war.'

'Oh, I'm so sorry, Your Majesty,' Alice squeezed Zina's hand, 'and for your poor mother.'

'We've tried to free her but failed,' the king said. 'She's well-guarded. We've had many ideas but none have worked. To agree to their demand is out of the question. When our people visit your world, we do no harm. We come to tell you about the destruction that's taking place in the oceans and to help you save them. The Dark Sea People, well, they are different. They want revenge on the humans for polluting the sea. They can't resolve a problem by peaceful means. With their evil ways they would spread disaster on land, believe me. They are warmongers and have always fought us.'

'You must be worried about the queen. But I have so many questions. What is the Land Adventure? Nor talked about it and then wished she hadn't. It must be a big secret. And how can you possibly visit our world? You're so tiny!'

Zina giggled, 'I can see that you're confused, Ally, but we can. We do visit your world, but we must prove to Father and his elders that we are worthy of this privilege. You see, we have a magic berry. The same as I gave you, it turns you into one of us. But it gives us the appearance of humans and we grow to your size. We take one for every day we spend on land. Our enemy wants the berry, but so far it remains our secret.'

'Yes, we want your people to understand more about the oceans, but we also come to learn,' the king added.

'If you haven't been to our world, Zina, how come you know so much?'

'Everyone going on the Land Adventure reports back to Father and I'm allowed to listen, as I'm the king's daughter.'

'I hope it will soon be your turn, Zina.'

'Yes, I will have earned it when the moon has been full twelve times. I want to visit your family and meet your brother.'

'It's impossible to think of you in our house. How can I explain who you are and where you come from? It will never work.' Alice shook her head.

'We'll think of something. But we've more urgent matters to attend to.'

'Oh, yes. Your mother! Can I do anything to help?'

'Yes, Ally, you can. Father and I have talked it over, and you might be able to rescue her. You'll have to do it in your human form though, and it could be dangerous. As one of us you can breathe under water, but how long can you hold your breath as a human and how deep can you dive?'

'I don't know, but I can practise.'

'Mother is held in the sea in your world, in a cage; one of those your people use to catch crabs. Once we distracted the guards long enough for two of our best swimmers to get up to the cage, but they couldn't get her out. As a human, with your size and strength, you shouldn't have a problem. By now they'll think we've given up, so we'll surprise them,' Zina said.

'Are there Portuguese men-of-war amongst the guards?' Alice chewed on her lip.

'I'm afraid so. The Dark Sea People have some on their side as well.' Zina hesitated and lowered her voice, 'That's why Father and I aren't sure we can ask you. Their sting could kill you.'

'Hmm,' Alice's brow furrowed, then cleared, 'I know, I'll get a wetsuit.'

'What's that?' Zina cut in.

'It's a suit made of rubber and if a jelly fish stings me, I'll still be all right.'

'Yes, I've seen people in them,' the king said, 'but have you got one?'

'No, but my friend Lizzy has and I'm sure I can borrow it. Course I'll help you.'

A deep sigh escaped the king and Zina's eyes shone. The king left his throne and swam in front of it. 'I'll describe the place where the Queen is held.'

The king put a small shell on the floor in front of her. 'This marks the cage. The guards are posted all around, but they aren't close.' He scattered small pebbles around the shell, some distance from it. 'You must dive inside the circle of guards, straight down on top of the cage; and quickly bring out the queen.' The king looked up at her, 'Any questions?'

'Why don't I just grab the cage and bring it up?'

'It's secured to the sea bed. We've tried. We managed to hook a line to it and fifty of our men pulled with all their strength, but the line broke. We were under attack at the time and had a few casualties.'

Alice nodded, 'I see, but what if the queen won't come with me? After all, I'm human and she doesn't know me.'

The king stroked his chin, 'You've got a point. It will be impossible to get a message to the queen now.'

'Ally will have to take me with her. Mother will know it's all right, when she sees me.' Zina said at once.

'That's too dangerous. If anything goes wrong I'd lose both of you.'

'You must let me, Father, nothing will go wrong. We must do it as soon as possible. Mother has been a prisoner for too long already.' Zina moved around in circles.

'Sit still, Zina!' her father urged.

'But we must hurry!'

Alice heard the urgency in Zina's voice, 'I'll have to practise my diving and holding my breath, and I must see Lizzy to borrow the wetsuit,' she protested.

'There is no time to lose. I'll take you back at

once and you can go and see your friend right away. I'll meet you tomorrow to find out how you're doing.' Zina pulled at Alice's arm as she was speaking.

Alice trembled, it's up to me now, she thought. Would she be able to save the queen?

## Chapter 11

# Simba the Spy

The door flung open as Alice put her hand on the doorbell. 'Hi, Ally, I saw you coming.' Lizzy threw her arms around her. 'Oh, your hair is wet. Been swimming again? Quite a water babe, aren't you!' Lizzy pulled away wiping her wet chin.

'Love it. That's why I'm here actually. Hope you don't think it's a cheek, but can I borrow your wetsuit for a day or two?'

'Course you can, I'll go and get it.'

A minute later Lizzy came down the stairs, jumping two steps at a time, her pigtails bouncing up and down. 'Here it is. Why do you want it? It's not that cold in the water.'

Bother, Alice thought, now I'll have to tell a lie. Every time I do something goes wrong. 'I'm learning to surf and I get cold spending time in the water. I keep on falling off. It's not easy, you know.'

'Super, I'm glad you're learning. We can go surfing together soon,' Lizzy beamed.

'Thanks, Lizzy, you're a lifesaver.' She doesn't know how true that is, Alice thought, and left with the wetsuit tucked under her arm.

Back in her room she struggled to get the suit on, it was a tight fit.

'What on earth are you wearing?'

She jumped and spun around. From behind the giant teddy bear, at the bottom of her bed, Simba's head stuck out. 'Oh, it's you. It's a wetsuit.' She told him about the kidnapping of the queen and how she was going to rescue her. 'Tomorrow morning I'll practise diving and holding my breath,' Alice said to finish.

'You're mad, absolutely mad,' Simba said.

'Why do you say that?'

'Cats stay away from water, we've got more sense.'

'Well, you're wrong and I'm not a cat, so there. I enjoy swimming and I want to help my friends. You could do with being more helpful. All you think about is yourself.'

'It's a cat's life.' Simba got up and stretched

leisurely, at the same time digging his claws into the duvet cover, 'I'm not complaining.'

'Don't do that, naughty cat!' Alice leaned forward to inspect the damage, luckily there wasn't any.

'Sorry, it's a habit,' Simba drawled. 'So what happens next?'

'I'll ask Joseph to help me tomorrow. It will be all right, you'll see.'

'Don't say I didn't warn you.' Simba disappeared behind the teddy bear as the door opened and Alice's mother came in.

'Are you talking to yourself, Alice? This is becoming a habit. Granny said she heard you chatting away in here earlier. You can ask Lizzy around anytime you like, she's a nice girl. You should spend more time with her.'

'It's OK, Mum, I saw her this afternoon.'

'Good. Dinner will be ready soon. What on earth are you wearing?'

'It's a wetsuit, Mum. I've borrowed it from Lizzy.'

'Oh well, take good care of it. You don't want to tear it.'

As soon as the door shut, Simba popped his head out, 'Thanks for not telling your mum that I'm here. You know what? I could tell you a thing or two about what's going on in this house.'

'What do you mean? Have you been spying?'

'Can't help overhearing things, can I? I heard Joseph and Tom talking about girls. You know, like girl friends.'

Alice sat straight up, 'Has Joseph got a girl friend? What's her name?'

Simba lifted one paw and studied it carefully before he answered, 'I think it's Geraldine, or it could be Pauline. Now let me see, it might even be Maxine. I know it ended in i-n-e.'

'Simba, you're impossible, and I didn't know you could spell. Anyway, Joseph doesn't know anyone with those names.'

'He does, he's taking her to the cinema tomorrow.'

'Come on, what's her name? I'll buy you some of your favourite treats.'

Simba's ears pricked up. 'Which ones, exactly?'

'You know, your very, very favourites.'

'How many?' Simba asked.

'A bag.'

'Would that be a bag a week, for a month?'

'Oh all right, but it will make you fatter,' Alice sighed.

'It's Geraldine, I remember now.'

'What about Tom, has he got a girl friend as well?'

'He didn't say. You like him, don't you, Ally?'

'Certainly not! You'd better leave now.'

Blushing, she pushed Simba off the bed.

'If you want me to leave, you'll have to open the door for me.'

'If you are so clever, jump up and push down the handle.'

'I have a little weight problem, which makes that hard, as you know,' Simba said.

She closed the door behind Simba and got out her diary. When she'd finished writing she crossed the landing and knocked on her brother's door, 'Can I come in?'

'What do you want?' Joseph sat at his desk, with his back to her, in front of his computer.

'Do I have to want something?' Alice hissed.

'Yeah, you do. What is it?'

'Are you going to the beach in the morning?'

'Think so. Why?' Joseph turned around and looked at her.

'I like to practise diving and holding my breath. You have a stop-watch, so I wonder if you could time me.'

'No can do, Sis.'

'Why not, I do favours for you.' Alice raised her voice.

'Sorry, Sis, busy,' came the short reply.

'I'll do it,' said a voice from behind her.

Alice twirled around. She hadn't seen Tom sitting in the corner. 'Oh, would you? Thanks.'

'What's this about then? A competition?' Tom grinned.

'No, I just need to know what I can do.'

'You'll have to dive off something. I'll borrow dad's dinghy and row you out.'

'Cool, thanks. Will ten o'clock be all right?'

'Sure.' Tom picked up his mobile and Alice fled the room, hoping that her blushes didn't show.

\*

The next morning, she found Tom leaning back in the dinghy waiting for her. He rowed out for about three hundred metres and stopped. 'Here should be deep enough. Did you bring the stop-watch?'

'Yeah, here it is.' Alice held up a see-through plastic bag. 'In case it gets splashed.' She stood up getting ready to dive, 'Tom, it's rocking too much. I can't keep my balance.'

'I'll try to steady it for you.'

'I'm losing my balance again.' She cried out and belly-flopped into the water with a big splash. Coming back up she hung on to the side, 'Can you give me a hand, please, Tom.'

She crawled back into the dinghy with Tom's help. Standing up she took several deep breaths and dived again. When she surfaced she saw the dinghy several metres away, and at the next moment a big wave hit her face. Alice coughed and spluttered, spitting out the salty water. Tom rowed over to her,

'Here take my hand.'

'I'm not doing very well, am I? This is hopeless! But I can't give up.' Alice blinked away the tears.

'Why is this upsetting you so much?' Tom wrinkled his forehead.

'It's important that's all.'

'But why? You said it wasn't a competition.' Tom scrutinized her face.

Alice ignored the question, 'How deep do you think it is here? And how long did my last dive take?'

'It took six seconds for you to come up, I'd say fairly deep. Here, try my goggles, they are better than yours.'

Her face lit up, 'Gee, thanks, Tom.'

The next dive lasted a few seconds longer, 'I can see much better with your goggles, Tom.'

'You're definitely improving.'

'Yes, and about time. I'm feeling more confident now.' Alice beamed.

Forty-five minutes later, Tom, who had made himself comfortable at the back of the dinghy, looked up from the stopwatch, 'You must really want to do this. I've lost count but I think you've dived a hundred times.'

'Don't be silly, not a hundred, but quite a few. That's enough! I'm tired. I must save my strength for the morning.'

'Why? What's happening tomorrow?'

'Oh, nothing. Nothing at all. Just another day,' she answered.

Tom shook his head and turned the dinghy around, heading back for shore. 'Kids,' he muttered.

Luckily Alice didn't hear him. 'Anyway, Tom, thanks a million, you are a star!'

'You're not bad yourself,' Tom grinned. Was it admiration she could hear in his voice? She hid a smile.

Back on the beach Joseph sat waiting for them. 'Your sister is really something, I've never seen anyone so determined,' Tom said, 'she's been diving for queen and country.'

'You're up to something, aren't you, Sis? Come on, tell me!' Joseph said.

'Tom is right.' Alice answered as she walked away. 'I've been diving for the queen and country,' and she said it with a smug smile, because it happened to be the truth.

Chapter 12

# The Rescue

At three o'clock that afternoon Alice returned to the beach, and swam out to meet Zina. 'I'm all set for tomorrow…' she began, but Zina interrupted her.

'You must do it now, Ally. There's no time to lose. Our spies have told us that Mother is being moved to deeper water, you wouldn't be able to reach her.'

'Are you sure? It just that…' But this was no time for hesitation. ''Course I'll come. It's lucky I put the wetsuit back on and I've still got Tom's goggles.'

'Good! A friend of mine is waiting further out to give us a lift. It's too far for you to swim.' She wanted to ask who the friend was, but Zina dived and she followed her flickering green scales just below the surface.

Suddenly a fin appeared and Alice saw the outline of a big fish. 'Is it a shark?' she shouted.

Zina swam back to her, 'No, it's Fino. He's a dolphin and very friendly. Hold on to his fin and he'll tow you, and he'll understand what you say to him.'

'Whoopee!' Alice cheered. She put her arm on the back of the dolphin, 'I've always wanted to do this. My friend Lizzy did when she was in Florida and I was so envious, this is a dream come true.' The dolphin turned his head to look at her. 'Look, Zina, he's smiling. He is friendly.'

'I told you.' Zina crept on to his back. 'Hang on, we're off!' Soon they skimmed across the water. After a time Fino slowed to a stop.

'Are we there?' Alice asked.

'No, I want to tell you of our plan. Father and his men are hiding in a shipwreck near by, ready to help. I'll send an emergency call if we need them. When you dive I'll hold on to the collar of your wet suit. I'll call out to Mother. She's been a prisoner for so long, she'll be weak. You might have to carry her up. Fino will be waiting and take us to Father. Any questions?'

Alice shook her head; it had happened too

quickly. No time to think, she thought, but I do have a "funny feeling" in my tummy about this.

'Right, we'll carry on slowly for the rest of the way. You must dive as soon as we get there. The longer we stay on the surface, the more likely they are to discover us. We must surprise the guards, or our rescue will fail. From this moment on we mustn't speak, our voices will carry and warn them.'

Alice took several deep breaths to fill her lungs with as much air as possible. Fino glided along, hardly disturbing the water. She was surprised that a dolphin could move so quietly. Then he stopped. Zina pointed downwards and swam on to her back, soon Alice felt her tugging at the collar.

She brushed aside the uncomfortable feeling of foreboding. Here we go! She took three deep breaths and dived.

Down and down she went, and now she was eager for the task ahead. The water cleared and a strange light appeared. In front of her she saw the two giant shells, which were the guard buildings, and the cage with a smaller shell inside it. Exactly the scene the king had shown her. Not far away lurked many Portuguese men-of-war.

A strong quiver went through the group of jellyfish. They had seen her! The hairs on her neck stood up.

Now the Portuguese men-of-war wobbled

forward, like lumps of milk jelly. She stifled a giggle, it looked funny. But she was scared! Acting quickly she grabbed hold of the cage and fumbled to find the opening. Seaweed swayed gently over the top and she brushed it away so that she could see inside. At last she got a clear view. Where was the queen? The shell inside the cage was empty!

'Mother, where are you?' Zina's desperate voice sounded by her left ear, 'We're too late! Mother is gone.'

Alice's heart sank, they had failed.

Zina left the safety of her shoulder and swam to the opening. 'Mother!' she screeched.

The guards caught sight of Zina and their tentacles moved faster, and faster. They floated forward in a rocking motion. Here was indeed a prize for them. They would be highly rewarded, if they captured the princess as well as the queen.

Alice decided that she had to save her friend instead. But she stopped and stared when Zina's mother emerged from behind the shell. A halo of light surrounded her, illuminating her pale green scales and her face framed by flaming red hair. The queen stretched out her arms towards her daughter. But the happiness on her face changed to anxiety, when she saw the advancing jellyfish.

By now Alice found it difficult to breathe. She pointed to her own mouth to signal to Zina that she needed air.

'Mother, you must swim to my friend!' Zina called out as she made her own way back to the collar of the wetsuit. Alice put out her hands and swept up the queen. She held her firmly and kicked off with her flippers. The jellyfish surrounded her but they hadn't yet covered her from above.

Air! Air! Her lungs screamed.

I must breathe! I'm dizzy! My only chance is to shoot straight up. But what's that? A man-of-war touched her shoulder and she glimpsed his tentacle close to her head. She glanced back.

Oh no! Zina's limp body was floating downwards. She had been stung! Had they killed her? Surely they wanted her alive? I'm on my own. I know that Zina hasn't sent a message to the king.

She reached the surface gulping for air. 'Fino, here, look after the queen. I have to go back for Zina, she's hurt.' Taking several deep breaths, she dived again. A mixture of thoughts whirled through her mind. What if the men-of-war had killed Zina? Too horrible! Was she too late? What if she'd saved the queen but lost her friend?

When she reached the bottom, she could see Zina's body surrounded by jellyfish. The fear rose inside her and for a split second she hesitated. Goose pimples pricked her arms, but she had to do this!

Go, Alice! Go! She urged herself. It's now or

never. She dived into the middle of the surprised jellyfish and grabbed Zina by her hair, pulling her away. The jellyfish attacked and circled her like a dozen inflated plastic bags bobbing up and down, lashing out with their tentacles, but her wetsuit protected her from their deadly stings. Gathering all her strength she vigorously flipped her feet together and pushed upwards, at the same time turning in a rotating movement. To her relief it propelled her towards the surface. With the advantage of speed she was soon clear. Wow, it worked! Amazing what you can do when you have to, she thought.

The queen's hands flew up to her mouth when she saw her daughter. Alice grabbed hold of the dolphin's fin with one hand, holding Zina close to her chest with the other. 'Quickly take us to the king!' Fino set off at speed and Alice found it hard to cling on, but cling on she did. Soon they reached the shipwreck in which the king and his men were waiting. Alice knew that the wreck was far too deep for her to dive to, 'Fino, take the queen to the king and come back for Zina, but be quick. I'll be all right. I'll tread water, whilst you're gone.'

'I'll not leave my daughter,' the queen protested.

'You must go with Fino, Your Majesty. Zina will be safe with me. Please, we must hurry.' The queen hesitated but then nodded. Fino moved his head up and down to let her know that he'd also understood.

Alice cupped her hands carefully lowering her friend into the water, so that she was floating protected by her hands. Zina, Princess of the Water People still hadn't moved.

Soon Fino appeared accompanied by the king, 'I don't know how to thank you, Ally, but that must come later. We have to return to the palace at once. Zina needs treatment for the sting.' The king looked down at the red bruise on his daughter's arm. 'We must hurry. Fino will take you back to your beach. We'll talk later. Goodbye for now.' The king gently took hold of Zina, his eyes full of sadness.

'Will she be all right?' Alice fought back the tears.

'I don't know,' the king answered.

Alice's voice quivered, 'Please hurry. Hurry!'

## Chapter 13

# What about Granny?

Fino brought her close to the beach avoiding the other swimmers. He swam slowly, gliding through the water, so that she didn't have to struggle to hang on. He knows that I am exhausted, she thought. She slid into the water but stayed, and rested her head on his side, gathering strength from his strong body, before she swam ashore.

On the beach she sat down on the hard pebbles. She struggled to remember every little detail about the rescue. It had happened so quickly. It had gone horribly wrong. When pictures of the unconscious Zina came into her mind, like a bad dream, she shook them off. I'm so tired, she thought, I'll never forget today. After a short rest she pulled off the wet suit and walked home, every step was an effort, her feet two heavy weights. She shivered with cold.

*

'Alice, you don't look well.' Granny pulled at some red wool; her tapestry by her side.

'Gran, I'm just tired.'

'Go and have a lie down. I'll bring you up a hot drink in a minute. You look all done in.'

Alice went to bed and gratefully drank the cup of hot chocolate which Granny brought her, after which she fell asleep and slept all through dinner.

She woke up with a start, 'Oh my goodness, it's nine o'clock in the evening!' Her first thought was for Zina. She prayed that her friend would be all right, but knew there was nothing she could do. Her tummy rumbled; she was starving. Going downstairs she could hear her mother and father in the kitchen. Something in the tone of her mother's voice made her stop on the last step. She couldn't help but listen in to the conversation.

'William, I'm really worried about Mum,' said her mother, 'today she told me she'd heard the cat talk. Do you think she's gone funny in the head?'

'You're kidding, Maggie. Did she really say that? But she seems perfectly sane to me, the fittest seventy years old I've ever known.'

'I know that's what makes it so strange.' Alice

could hear that her mother was worried.

'What did you say to her?' her father asked.

'I said, "surely you must be wrong."'

'And then?'

'Oh, I don't know what to make of it, William. She squinted at me in a funny way and shook her head. We left it at that, but I've noticed how she's looking at Simba. It's weird.'

'Oh no,' Alice scowled, 'where is he, the horrid cat? He isn't allowed to talk to anyone else.' She crept upstairs, forgetting how hungry she was, and found Simba sitting on the landing.

'I want a word with you,' she hissed.

'Good, I want to know about your diving lesson. Will you be able to rescue the queen tomorrow?'

'I did that today, I had to,' Alice answered grumpily, 'but I'll tell you about that later. This is serious.' Simba's ears pricked up as Alice continued, 'Mum and Dad think that Gran has gone bonkers and it's your fault. You've talked to her! Simba, how could you?' She felt her face getting hot and knew that red spots had appeared on her cheeks.

'Only a couple of times.' Simba looked at the ceiling.

'More than once! That's worse.' Alice flung out her arms in an angry gesture.

'I didn't say much.'

'What did you say? Simba, please tell me!'

'The first time I said, nice day today.'

'And what did Granny say?'

'She said, yes isn't it lovely. Then she spun around and gawked at me. You should've seen the look on her face. It was worth a saucer of cream.'

'Oh Simba,' Alice groaned, 'and then?'

'Nothing, I didn't say anything else.'

'And Granny, what did she do?'

'She kept on looking at me and opened her mouth, as if to say something, but shut it again. Then she shook her head and went out into the garden.'

'And the second time?' Alice held her breath.

'I said the same thing, only this time she didn't answer.'

'Where were you?'

'In the conservatory, both times.'

'And was the window open?'

'Pretty sure it was.' Simba held up one paw and studied it carefully.

'Perhaps we can explain it by saying it was someone else talking in the garden,' Alice suggested.

'OK, whatever you say. I like Granny. No big deal. If it upsets her, I won't do it again.'

'No, you won't! If you do, I'll use my next wish to undo your talking.'

'You wouldn't. You like that I can talk, too much.' Simba licked his paw seemingly unconcerned.

'Suppose you're right. Well then, I'll ask Mum

to put you on a diet. You're too fat.'

'You wouldn't!' Simba's paw flew open, claws showing.

'You bet! And you wouldn't dare scratch me! I don't want Gran upset for all the talking cats in the world. Do you hear me?' Simba didn't answer, but put his paw in front of his mouth, claws withdrawn, to indicate that he wasn't talking.

*

The next morning as Alice poured milk into a bowl of cereal, Granny came into the kitchen. 'You look much better, Alice.'

'Yeah, but I'm starving, I missed my dinner last night. How are you? Are you all right?' She examined her granny's face.

'I'm fine. Why shouldn't I be? Have you seen Simba this morning?'

'No not yet. Why do you want him, Gran?' Alice dropped the spoon into the bowl with such force that milk splattered over the table.

'Just asking.' Granny fetched the dishcloth from the sink and handed it to her. 'I think he looks a lot like Garfield; you know that cat they made a film about. I wonder if Simba is as clever as him. What do you think?'

'I doubt it.'

'Well, I'll just go and see if I can find him.'

Alice put her bowl of cereal on the sideboard and

ran after her. Better not leave her alone with Simba, I don't trust him, she thought. 'I'll help you to find him, Granny. He might be in the conservatory, he likes it there.'

Sure enough, they found Simba sleeping on one of the padded cushions under the open window. Granny lifted him up and sat down with him on her lap. Simba's tail swung from side to side and he tried to jump off, but Granny held him down.

'You stay here with me for a little while.' Granny tightened her grip on him. 'Go and finish your breakfast, Alice, you said you were hungry.'

Alice gave Simba a stern look and when he put a paw in front of his mouth, she knew he wouldn't speak. 'Sure, Gran, I'll see you.'

Later Simba was waiting outside her room. 'You'll never guess,' he said as soon as they were inside Alice's room, 'Gran is trying to make me talk.'

Alice giggled nervously, 'You didn't though, did you?'

'Course not, not after all your threats.'

'Poor Gran, I'm sure she'll give up, thinking she's been mistaken.'

*

But Granny didn't give up. In the coming days Alice often found Simba on Granny's lap. One afternoon Simba blocked the way, as she was hurrying upstairs, 'Psst! Can I have a word?'

Alice had a quick scan around to make sure no one was about. 'Not now, I'm upset. I've been to the beach every afternoon for three days, but no sign of Zina. I'm worried, suppose she doesn't get well. I might never see her or the Water People again.' She wiped her eyes with the back of her hands.

'I'm sorry about Zina, but I must talk to you. It's Granny, she won't leave me alone. She insists that I speak to her and she is offering me all sorts of treats.'

'And you take them?'

'Course I do. Silly not to. She'd think I was ill, if I didn't. Then she'd get your mum to take me to the vet and you know how much I like that.'

'But you didn't speak to her?'

'Course not, I promised, didn't I? But this has got to stop. I have to think about my weight. You know how weak I am, I can't say no to a treat. Besides I can't spend my days sitting on Granny's lap. I'm bored. I need exercise.'

'Hmm, I agree, we have to think of a plan.' Alice concentrated, 'I know, tomorrow when Gran picks you up, I'll walk past the open window. I'll say; it's a nice day today, isn't it?'

'What if it isn't?'

'What if it isn't what?' Alice asked.

'A nice day, of course.'

'Well, then we'll have to wait until it is.' Alice

snorted, her mouth pinched.

'What if the window isn't open?'

'Simba, don't make things more difficult than they are. I'll make sure the window is open.'

'Oh, all right, but the plan has got to be foolproof. I know it won't work. You have to sound like me.'

'I can do that. Listen! My name is Simba.' Alice drawled.'

'Do I really sound like that? Quite, so, so …'

'Lazy?' Alice filled in. 'Yeah, you do. Take my word for it.'

'I was going to say "laid back" actually,' Simba said.

*

The following morning Alice waited until her granny was seated in the conservatory with Simba on her lap. Walking past the window where Granny could see her, she drawled in Simba's voice, 'It's a nice day today, isn't it?'

Granny looked from Alice to Simba and then back again. 'Why did you speak like that? Have you done it before?'

'Yes, I might have. It's handy to speak with another voice, like in our school plays. That's why I've been practising.'

'I see, but last time I couldn't see you.'

'I don't know, Gran, perhaps I was just walking past and you missed me.'

'I don't think so, but I can't be sure.' Granny shook her head and put Simba back on the floor. 'Alice, are you absolutely...? No forget it, it was nothing.' Granny leaned back and deep lines appeared on her forehead.

Simba took the opportunity to shoot out into the garden, followed by Alice. 'Thanks, I think it worked,' Simba purred and rubbed up against her leg.

'I'm not so sure. Gran is no fool, but we'll know soon enough.'

Chapter 14

# How Much does Granny Know?

Alice floated on her back, gently moving her arms to keep her balance in the water. On the beach Joseph and a dark haired girl were playing with a beach ball. The ball landed in the sea and Alice turned over to catch it and throw it back to them. Who was that girl? Then her thoughts returned to Zina. I must have news soon or I'll go mad. At that moment she felt a light touch on her leg. 'Ana, it's you! What a surprise!'

'Fino brought me. I needed his help to find your beach. I've never been to your world; it's an honour for me. The king said that I should take the message to you, as I'm Zina's best friend.' Alice felt a pang of jealousy, but then she thought, Lizzy is my best friend, so it's only fair.

'Zina is very ill, but she will recover. We know you care, and we're sorry we've kept you waiting for news,' Ana said.

'Please, take me to her.'

'Sorry, Ally, but I can't. The Dark Sea People are furious to have lost their hostage. We've been expecting an attack for days. It has been too dangerous to come sooner.'

'Ana, you're so brave, I'm so glad you've come. I've been worried sick.'

'You deserve it. You became an important person to us when you saved the queen and Zina. The trouble is...' Ana squirmed.

'What is it, Ana? Tell me!'

'No, I mustn't. It's better if the king tells you himself.'

'Is it bad news?'

'I always get into trouble for talking too much.'

'But I must see Zina,' Alice insisted.

'I'll find out if it's possible. Perhaps Fino can take you to meet the king. He can bring you to us safely. You'll need a guarded escort.'

'Why do I need guards?'

'Oops, here I go again talking too much. I'll have to go, but be here as usual and be prepared.'

Ana dived before Alice had chance to answer.

*

'Good, am I glad to see you,' Alice said, when later she found Simba waiting outside her door. She picked him up and carried him in, 'Gosh, you weigh a ton!'

'Well, put me down then!'

Alice dropped him on the bed, where he landed with a thump, 'Listen to this!' She told him about the meeting with Ana.

'I don't like the sound of that. Don't go!'

'Course I will, I can't wait to see Zina. Anyway is Gran all right?'

'Think so, she hasn't bothered me since this morning.' Simba hung his head.

'I thought you'd be pleased.'

'Yeah, me too, but I was beginning to like it. She's nice. She used to scratch me behind the ears. I miss it, and the treats.

'You're a hopeless cat, you really are,' Alice sighed.

*

That evening with the whole family around the dinner table, Joseph faced his granny,

'You're quiet, Gran.'

Granny didn't answer but gave him a tiny smile. Then she abruptly turned to her daughter. 'Remember, Maggie, when I told you that I'd heard

Simba talk? Well, now I know that it was Alice all along. She was outside the window.'

A grin spread across Joseph's face, 'Granny, did you really think you'd heard Simba talk? That's news to me.'

'I guess your mother didn't want to spread it around. Yes, I did, but I'm sure now that I was mistaken.' She shrugged her shoulders.

'That's all right, Maud, only you seemed so certain. You had us worried,' Alice's father said.

'No need for that, William.'

Alice sighed with relief, it had worked. But when Granny winked at her, Alice's smile froze. Her thoughts racing: How much does Granny know?

*

Lizzy had been invited to lunch the next day and after a morning's windsurfing, the girls made their way back to Alice's home. 'We're eating in the garden, Lizzy. We're having salad,' Alice's mother said.

Granny indicated to Alice and Joseph, 'Come and sit next to me. It's nice of you to give up wind surfing time for me.'

'Well, I want to see you before you go,' Joseph said. 'And I've promised to help Mum in the garden this afternoon.'

'Can't you stay longer, Granny?' Alice asked. Must find out what she knows, she thought.

'No, my sweetheart, I'm off to the conference.

It's all about saving marine life.'

'Wish I could help. I know it's important,' Alice said.

'But you can! Get some of your friends together and pick up rubbish from the beach, especially the plastic bags blowing about. They're found in the stomachs of seals, whales and turtles. Kills them! They mistake the plastic bags for jelly fish and die.'

'That's gross!' Alice cried out. 'But Granny's idea about cleaning the beach is brill. What do you think, Lizzy?'

'Mega! Let's suggest it to Mrs Brown at school. The whole class could go,' Lizzy answered.

'Thank you, girls, how marvellous!' Granny smiled and patted Alice's hand, 'It would make such a difference to the wild life and us, if everyone could take their litter home. It's not a hard thing to do.'

'I often see it near bins. Some people think the next metre is too far to walk.' Alice's mother held out a plate to Lizzy, 'Beetroot?'

'No thanks.' Lizzy wrinkled her nose and turned to Granny, 'Please, tell us more about saving the sea.'

'Well, it would make a huge difference if more Marine Reserves could be created. Everything inside would be protected and the seabed would have a chance to recover, especially where dredging has taken place.'

'What's dredging?' Joseph and Lizzy asked in

chorus, and then smiled at each other.

'The harvesting of scallops is one reason. It causes dreadful destruction. The seabed is scraped of every living thing, leaving it completely dead. Delicious as they are, I'll only eat scallops, which have been certified as picked by divers,' Granny said.

'I'm taking Granny to the station after lunch,' Alice's mother said, changing the subject.

'I'm sorry to leave, but I'll be back soon. I'll miss you all. You too, Simba!' Granny bent down to stroke Simba, who was to be found by her feet most of the time.

'Do you want to take Simba home with you, Mum?'

Alice nearly knocked over her glass of mango juice. Her mother's eyebrows shot up, 'Only a joke, Alice.'

'I know what he means to you, I'd never take him away.' Granny had that "funny look" on her face again, "that look" which Alice couldn't explain.

Later as Granny left for the station, she hugged Alice and whispered into her ear, 'Don't look so worried. Your secret is safe with me.'

'I don't know what you mean, Granny.'

'Oh, I'm sure you do, Alice. I'm sure you do.'

Chapter 15

# Alice Becomes a Princess

At three o'clock precisely Alice was back in the water. She felt a tug and looked down to see Ana hanging on to her big toe with both arms. 'The king has agreed to your visit. Fino is waiting further out, where he can't be seen. He'll tow us to the king.'

Soon Alice and Ana were skimming across the surface clinging onto Fino's fin. When he slowed down she saw what looked like a small island floating on the water. It was the king and a dozen of his men, all of them carrying spears. Stingrays were guarding them. Alice knew they were there to help, but she avoided getting too close. The stingrays parted to let Alice and Ana into the circle. Why did the king look so serious? Was Zina worse?

'How is Zina, Your Majesty?' she asked reaching for the small berry in the king's hand.

'Not well, she sleeps most of the time, but your visit will do her good. We're above our forest here, so we'll dive straight down.' Alice followed the king closely as they dived, with the stingrays forming a protective circle around them.

The queen was waiting by the palace gate eager to greet Alice. 'I'm fully recovered, thanks to you, but Zina isn't well. I'll take you to her without delay.'

Zina was lying on a blue coloured blade of seaweed, attached at either end by twined grass; it was rocking gently to and fro like a hammock. Her copper-red hair spread out above her head, her face pale and eyes closed. Alice bit her lip, I must be brave for Zina's sake, she thought. She took her hand, 'Zina, it's me. Please wake up, don't sleep anymore! I miss you so much.'

Zina's eyelids flickered and slowly she opened her eyes, 'Ally, good to see you. How are you?' she whispered.

'I'm fine, and you must get well.' Realizing that Zina was still seriously ill, Alice forced a smile and gently squeezed her hand.

'I'm sorry, Ally, but your visit must be short. Zina needs rest, and the king wants to talk to you. Come with me,' the queen said. Together they swam to the big hall where the king was waiting.

'Ally,' he began, 'we want to thank you for rescuing the queen and Zina. I am going to give you the title of Honorary Princess.'

'Me a princess!' Alice gaped.

The king continued, 'But by your good deed, I'm afraid we've placed you in great danger. Many more Dark Sea People than usual are coming up from the darkness of the deep. We are sure it's because of you. We believe they want revenge and that you're now on their most wanted list.'

'We'll do all we can to protect you,' the queen added.

'They are our only enemy, but there are many dangerous creatures in the sea willing to help them,' the king said.

'So they really are angry with me.' An anxious frown showed on Alice's face.

'I don't want to scare you, but you must be aware of the danger.' The king held up his hand. 'But enough! Let's talk of happier times. The Water People will have a celebration in this hall as soon as Zina is well. It will be a big party and we'll make you a princess.'

'Thank you, Your Majesties.' She turned from the king to the queen. 'I'm just pleased that I was able to help.'

*

In the coming week Alice enjoyed her summer holiday by spending time with Lizzy, either windsurfing or just playing on the beach. She also met Ana, who gave her progress reports of Zina's recovery. It was good news, day by day her health improved. One day Zina herself was there to meet her, doing somersaults to prove that she was truly well.

'Ally, we've arranged the celebration in your honour, it's the day after tomorrow.'

*

On the day of the party Fino brought Alice to where Zina and the guards were waiting. Arriving at the palace she could see that it had been decorated with garlands of sea plants. In the big hall hundreds of pretty corals sparkled on the walls. All the Water People were there and as soon as they saw Zina and Alice they clapped hands.

The girls swam up to the giant shell where the king and the queen sat side by side.

'Do as I do,' Zina said, 'when we reach Father and Mother, we'll flip our feet up in the air with our heads facing down. We call it the "Royal Flip". It's protocol on occasions like this. It's to show respect for the king and queen. Only royalty is greeted in this way.' Alice hid a smile, and did the flip without falling over.

The king stood up and began to speak, 'Ally, you are here to receive the highest honour my kingdom can give. When you leave this room you will be a princess of the Water People. You will be known as Princess Ally.'

Zina whispered, 'Do the flip again when Father holds up his hand. Only this time stay like it, until he tells you to get up.'

Alice struggled really hard to keep her balance and couldn't hear what the king was saying. He appeared to be reading from a leaf and after what seemed an eternity, he placed his hand on her head.

'Arise, Princess Ally,' the king proclaimed in a loud voice.

The Water People cheered as they greeted their new princess. Her head was spinning but she wasn't sure if it was because she'd been standing on it, or that she was now a princess. Zina rushed up and hugged her and the queen kissed her cheek.

'We have another daughter,' the king said.

'We do indeed,' the queen answered, 'and now the party will begin. Let's move into the garden, where the festivities and food are waiting for us.'

The food was laid out on floating fronds and what a choice! Alice recognized the purple plums and the royal pears. Different coloured kelp was neatly stacked on top of each other forming a tower, also barnacles in their hard shells, and sea-worms. To her horror the worms wriggled, still alive. Ooh! I could never ever eat those, even if I was starving, she thought. She saw whelks, mussels, oysters and shrimps, also the cucumber looking thing, which oozed with yellow stuff when bitten into. Yuk! But most of the food she hadn't seen before. The Water People swam from frond to frond, tucking into the goodies. Many popped snails into their mouths, they were very popular. Just as well I'm not hungry, there isn't anything here I fancy. Even the fruit tastes fishy, Alice thought.

Zina and Alice swam amongst the Water People, who all wanted to meet her. Oh dear, I'd no idea that it's such hard work being a princess, she thought. Time after time she told the story of the rescue. Ana and her sister Nor, as well as Silla and Haja, were proud to know their new princess. Alice met so many of their friends; she got dizzy again, just trying to remember their names.

A young man followed them at a distance as they moved around the garden. She glanced back at him. He had dark hair and eyes, and his body was covered in copper coloured scales. Lines in a lighter shade went down the sides of his legs, making him stand out from the others.

'Who is he, Zina?' Alice whispered.

'That's Sal, a good friend. Come on let's talk to him.' Zina swam up to Sal, 'Princess Ally would like to meet you.' Sal bowed to her.

'Please don't..,' Alice began.

'Our people will bow to you.' Zina interrupted and then continued, 'Will you look after Ally for me, Sal? I'll be back soon.'

'Am I the first human you've met?' Alice asked.

'Yes, I haven't been on my Land Adventure yet. Tell me, are all humans as brave and as pretty as you are?'

Blushing she answered, 'Well, yes, quite a few. It depends. Isn't it the same here in your world?'

'Yeah, we're not all the same. For example, not everyone wants to go on the Land Adventure so they don't try to earn it. But for me it will be an achievement. I have an older brother; his name is Link. Has Zina mentioned him?'

'No, she hasn't, but so much happens when we meet, we've hardly got time to talk.'

'Link is also Zina's friend. He is hoping to go on the Land Adventure with her.'

'And when is your turn, Sal?'

'Many moons will have to pass, but I would like to meet you in your world.'

'Can't wait,' Alice's heart skipped a beat. She'd just realized that she could have visits from the Water People in the future. She would be able to help and advise them.

'Will you come back soon?' Sal asked.

'As often as I can, I love seeing all the wonderful things you have here.'

'That's great,' Sal laughed, 'but aren't you worried about the Dark Sea People? They are looking for you.'

'Really? Are you sure?' Alice frowned. Should she be afraid?

At that moment Zina returned. 'Come on, Ally, our people have put on a show for you. You'll be amazed.'

'Bye then, see you soon,' Sal bowed. It's going to be hard to get used to this bowing, Alice thought.

'Do you like him?' Zina asked as they sat down to watch the show.

'Mm. He's cool, and he told me about Link. What's he like?'

'He's older that Sal and just as nice. He's also our best swimmer and Father often sends him on dangerous missions.'

'Like what?' To her disappointment Zina shook her head.

'Can't say. Shush! The show is starting.'

Alice clapped her hands, her eyes like saucers. This was all done for her. The Water People did acrobatics and incredible dives from great heights. Alice laughed when she saw fishes swim through hoops. She nudged Zina, 'Did your people see this on land?'

'Yes, that's where most of their ideas come from. Our people are good, aren't they?'

'It's an underwater circus! It's mega.' Alice clapped her hands until they hurt. 'I love this, Zina. It's brilliant, but I've been here for ages. My family will be terribly worried. Perhaps they'll think I've drowned.'

'Don't panic, Ally. It seems a long time to you, but it's no more than half an hour in your world. It's time for us to leave anyway. I will come with the guards as far as the forest, where Fino will be waiting to take you back to your beach. By the way, he'll be keeping an eye on you from now on.'

'I see, but why?'

'Ally, you must take the threat from the Dark Sea People seriously. We do. Father won't allow you to come for a while. It's safer that way.'

'Oh no! But ...' Alice stopped abruptly. Zina's taut face and unsmiling eyes, told her that she had no choice but to accept the king's decision.

*

'You know what,' Alice said to Fino as she clung onto his fin on the way home. 'I'd like to swim and play with you. That would be so much fun. It's always been a dream of mine. Perhaps one day?' Fino nodded his head vigorously. 'Great, that means *yes*, doesn't it? You've promised!' Fino nodded again and before he swam away he put a wet nose on her cheek. He had given her a kiss!

Chapter 16

# Fino and Alice
# Become Celebrities

Alice met Lizzy on the beach the next day as usual. The sun shone from a clear blue sky, and Alice wiped the sweat from her forehead. The girls stuck an umbrella into the pebbles to give them shade. The sun had brought out a band of freckles across Lizzy's cheeks and nose. Suddenly Alice realized who her friend reminded her of, 'Lizzy, you look like Pippi Longstocking, what with your pigtails and all.'

'I what?' Lizzy laughed, 'I wish I was as super strong as she is.' Lizzy patted the sun bed she was unfolding.

'You've read the book then?' Alice asked.

'Yeah, it was one of my favourites, when I was little.'

'Me too.' Alice nodded.

Lizzy had helped to carry the beds from the house, so they didn't have to lie on the hard stones. The girls had also brought sandwiches for lunch.

Joseph and Tom spent most of the morning wind surfing. Joseph kept an eye on his sister. Alice saw him glancing in their direction several times and now he was coming over, followed by Tom.

'Got my sandwiches, Sis?'

'Here! Have you got any, Tom?' Alice waved a cheese sandwich in front of Tom, eager for him to take it.

'Have one of mine as well,' Joseph said.

'Are you sure? Thanks.' Tom sat down on the pebbles and got out his mobile. 'Just telling Mum I won't be home for lunch,' then he continued, 'you know, there's a dolphin out there. It's unusual so close to shore. Could be it's such a hot summer.'

'Really?' Lizzy said. 'Let's go and take a look.'

'I'm not sure we should. We might frighten him.' Alice knew it was Fino.

Lizzy insisted, 'I'll go on my own if you don't come.'

'All right,' Alice said reluctantly.

The girls steered their boards towards the dolphin. Alice got to him first and as she bent down to stroke his smooth skin, she whispered, 'Ask Zina when I can come again.' In a loud voice she shouted, 'Come closer, Lizzy, he'll let you touch him.'

'Is it safe? He is wild after all,' Lizzy didn't move.

'I'm pretty sure this is a tame dolphin, perhaps he's escaped from a sanctuary. Look how friendly he is. He is definitely smiling.'

Lizzy moved close and touched Fino. 'You're right, this is brill.'

'Let's go in with him, I'll go first. Hang onto my board.' Alice slid into the water; Fino had come to play with her. He was keeping his promise.

Alice clung on to Fino's fin and he set off at speed towing her. When they got back Alice shouted, 'Your turn, Lizzy, hang on to his fin like I did. It's great fun!'

Lizzy clung on, but after a few metres she lost her grip. 'I want to try again,' she shouted, and this time she held on tight. Both girls shrieked with laughter when Fino rolled over and over and did somersaults. Lizzy screamed when he disappeared and came up under them, it was so unexpected.

Not surprisingly their games had been noticed from the beach. Joseph and Tom rowed out in the dinghy and were soon followed by surfers. Alice whispered to Fino, 'Shouldn't you leave now?' But Fino shook his head; he was clearly enjoying the attention. He played with Joseph and Tom, and the other surfers, but he repeatedly came back to Alice. He only allowed her to ride on his back.

'Sis, the dolphin likes you. I'm jealous.' Joseph said after he'd failed to get onto Fino's back.

Tom gave her admiring glances. 'You are great with him, Ally,' he said, with a big grin.

*

The next day saw a repeat performance and the day after that. By now the media had been informed and to Alice's amazement a television crew turned up. It was obvious to everyone that the dolphin preferred her and only did certain tricks with her.

'Why does the dolphin always come to you?' the reporter inquired. 'He's a friend and he trusts me,' Alice answered jokingly, and that is what everyone thought it was: a joke. That evening Alice and Fino were on the local news.

Alice's mother, who had heard about the dolphin, was nevertheless astounded to see her daughter on TV. Granny phoned. 'It was magic to watch,' she said. Why had Granny used the word magic?

When Alice's father came home, he waved the local evening paper. 'Look at this, Maggie, our daughter is on the front page.'

'She's been on telly as well, William. Can I see the paper?' There was a picture of Alice and Fino and the caption read: Girl On A Dolphin. It described how the dolphin favoured this girl and how curious it was. The reporter even interviewed a marine expert to ask him if he could explain this phenomenon. He'd answered that it was fairly usual for a dolphin to befriend a particular person.

'You're a celebrity, Sis.' Joseph couldn't help looking impressed.

*

Later in Alice's room Simba said, 'Wow, this is cool. I saw you on the telly. It was brave of you to say he's a friend.'

'I was only telling the truth, I knew no one would believe me. I don't like to lie, but it's difficult, as I can't tell anyone about Zina and the Water People.'

'Best say nothing then, Ally.'

'I know, but what do I say to Mum and Dad and Joseph when I disappear to visit Zina?'

'You could say you've gone for a walk on the beach.'

'That would be a lie though. Wouldn't it?'

'Not if you go on a walk first.'

'See what you mean, suppose I could call it a white lie. But you're only meant to tell them, so not to hurt someone's feelings. That's meant to be kinder, you know.'

'You've a problem, Ally. Fame doesn't come easy, now that you're a princess as well as a celeb.'

'I know I'm not a real princess, but I am to the

Water People. Now I'm going to write in my diary, you can stay if you stop chatting.'

But after a few minutes there was a knock on the door, 'Can I come in, Sis?'

'If you must.'

'Ally, that dolphin really behaves as if he knows you. It's freaky. When you talked to him, I think he understood you.'

'Dolphins are very intelligent.'

'I know, but it's freaky just the same.' Joseph shrugged his shoulders.

Alice was keen to change the subject. 'Who was that girl I saw you with on the beach?'

'What girl?'

'Don't pretend you don't know. You seemed really keen, the way you were messing about.'

'Just playing with a ball, that's all.'

'What's her name? No, let me guess. Say I get it right in three guesses.' Alice noticed that Simba sat up, looking very alert. She smiled at him and turned back to her brother. This was going to be interesting.

'If you guess it, I'll give you the loan of my board all day tomorrow,' Joseph was confident.

'Deal! I guess it ends with i-n-e.'

Joseph opened his mouth but closed it again without saying anything.

'I guess Maxine.'

'Wrong.'

'Well then, how about Pauline?'

'Wrong.' Joseph's eyes were narrowing.

'Let's say Geraldine, and you've taken her to the cinema.' Alice triumphed.

'You knew that all along. I shall have a word with Tom; he's got no business telling you.' Joseph stamped his foot.

'I swear it wasn't Tom. Honestly!'

'He's the only one who knows, I thought he was my mate. The board deal is off.' Joseph stomped out of the room.

'Oh dear, I've got Tom into trouble as well. I wish I hadn't said anything. Simba, perhaps it's not a good idea you telling me stuff.'

'What a mess,' Simba said. 'Now we'll have to sort this one out. You should think before you speak.'

Alice couldn't believe her ears, 'You're a fine one to talk. You got us into the last one and this one as well, come to think of it.'

'So it's my fault? You were the one to talk this time!'

'But if you hadn't said anything, I wouldn't have known anything.' Alice paced the floor, 'But I suppose we're both to blame. Sorry!' She sat down next to him.

'I'm glad we are friends again.' Simba purred and snuggled up to her.

*

A thunderstorm woke Alice during the night but it had cleared by the morning and she set off to meet Fino. The other surfers followed immediately, staying close to her, knowing that as soon as Alice went into the water the dolphin would come. She couldn't get away even for a minute.

By Fino's side she whispered to him, 'See what's happening! You mustn't show yourself. I'll be here when no one is about, the time we call six o'clock in the morning. Bring Zina, I must speak to her.'

Fino dived with a flip of his tail and Alice swam to the beach. The other surfers called for her to come back, but she shook her head.

Chapter 17

# Alice Learns Magic

Alice crept downstairs dressed in her swimsuit. She slid the veranda door open and heard it click shut behind her. She was locked out! Bother! It can't be helped, I have to hurry, she thought. Although it was August it was still cold this early in the morning. She shivered, as she lifted the latch on the garden gate.

'I can guess where you are going.' It was Simba's lazy drawl.

'Simba, you made me jump. Have you been out all night?'

'Yep, the flap is locked.'

'I did ask Dad to check.'

'I know. I heard you. He still forgets.'

'Well, I'm locked out as well, but I must rush. See you!'

Alice waded into the sea, wondering if this was a good idea after all. It was so cold. She was covered in goose pimples. She rubbed her arms hard and quickly dived into the water. She could see Fino's fin further out and swam towards it. Once there she was pleased to see Zina waiting by his side. 'This is the only time I can come now, because of the publicity.' Alice said.

'I know, Fino has explained everything. You'll have to be careful until this has blown over. Did anyone see you go into the water?' Zina asked.

'No, the beach huts hide the view from the houses and at home no one will miss me. They are asleep. Can I come with you?'

'All right, Ally, but it could be dangerous. The Dark Sea People are still looking for you.'

When they reached the Forest Gate, Zina stopped. 'Pay attention, Ally, I will show you how to find the opening. Look here where the red algae is growing, next to the clumps of brown kelp.' Zina pointed, 'Push down on the brown kelp and it will give way and let you in. You go first this time.'

Alice leaned against the slimy kelp and pushed hard, it was surprisingly strong and bendable, but suddenly it gave way and she fell into the forest.

Once inside, she again had the feeling of being watched. She was right. She caught a glimpse of the black fish with the long hairy moustache disappearing behind a weed. A second later her feet were ensnared. Before she had time to be scared, she instinctively jerked her legs up and down and felt the grip loosen. Looking back she could see a trail of black hairy streamers unwinding from her feet.

Zina turned with dismay on her face. 'Well done, Ally. I know who that was. Let's hurry away from here. Father told me to bring guards. He won't be pleased to hear that I didn't.'

But when the two girls arrived by the palace wall, a huge octopus blocked the way.

'Is he one of ours?' Alice called out.

'No! Quickly, shoot straight up and get away from his tentacles,' Zina yelled, her clear voice was razor sharp.

It startled Alice. This must be serious! Hurriedly she got ready to flip into an upward spin.

She couldn't see! Only darkness! Black water was everywhere.

She thrashed about, 'Zina!'

The horrible stuff got into her mouth. She spat! She could feel it in her hair and her eyes. Disorientated she could no longer control her movements. I'm going to die, she thought. Then she felt a strong grip on her arm and she was pulled along. The octopus had got her!

'Oh, help me!' she'd cried and realized that she could see again. Below her floated the black ink cloud that had engulfed her. Zina's strong arms had pulled her up and away, it wasn't the octopus tentacles.

'I guess we are quits now. Thanks for saving me. That was scary.' Alice tried to wipe the stuff off her face with shaking hands.

Zina started to laugh seeing Alice's black streaky face. But then she became serious, 'Father will be furious with me.'

He was. The king exploded, 'Where were the guards?' he roared. Zina flinched and looked away from her father. Although the king was kind, Alice knew that he wasn't to be trifled with. Zina was the only person to disobey him and get away with it, but sometimes even she felt his anger.

The king turned to Alice, 'It's clear that I must give you power to protect yourself. I will transfer strong magic to you. Close your eyes and be ready to receive it.' Soon the king spoke, 'It's done! Now you'll be able to speak to all sea creatures even in your human form. There's more for you to learn, but Zina will show you. You mustn't misuse the power Ally, but I think you're clever enough to realize that.'

Alice opened her eyes expecting to feel different, because of the magic, but she didn't. 'I understand,

Your Majesty, and thank you so much.' She did a flip to show her respect.

The queen smiled. 'Now go with Zina to her room, you both need to wash off the ink.'

Once inside the small chamber, Zina brought her a shell filled with a green jelly and a sea sponge. 'Here, this is what we use to clean ourselves.'

'What is it?'

'It's a blend of planktons and oysters, works a treat. It oils your skin as well and keeps it healthy.'

Alice watched as Zina rubbed herself with the mixture and followed her example. She grimaced, 'It stinks and it's leaving my hair and face green.'

'It will wear off. Now sit down and listen carefully. I repeat what Father said, you must never misuse this power.'

'I promise. Cross my heart,' Alice said solemnly.

'Right then, I'm going to teach you magic. If you need to hide or if you are in danger say: Sea cape attach to me.'

'What will happen?'

'You'll be covered by a camouflage cape and from above you'll look like a flounder fish.'

'Wow, that's cool!'

'There's more, Ally. I have this ring for you. It will only be on your finger when you're one of us. It has a green stone, which changes colour according to your surroundings. If you see the stone turn red, you must rub it immediately. It will send a signal that you're in danger. We call it the rainbow ring.'

Alice slipped the ring onto her finger. 'Can I really do all this? I can't wait to try it out. I'll never let you down! I will keep the secret of the berries and help to protect them! I'd rather die than tell anyone about you and the Water People.'

'We are also giving you berries to take with you, so you can come and visit us. But you must let Fino know first so that we can send guards to meet you.'

'But where do I keep the berries?'

'You have a small pocket under your scales, just there.' Zina pointed.

Alice ran her finger under the scales, 'Oh yes, how funny!'

Zina smiled, 'Yes, I keep a small dagger in my pocket for protection. But come on, Princess Ally, let's swim out and meet the people.'

They met Ana, and Nor; both gave her a big hug. Many of the Water People greeted her as their princess by doing the flip, which made her giggle. Zina gave her a sharp elbow. 'Now you're a princess, you'll have to behave like one. It's what's expected of you.'

'Sorry, it looks comical. By the way, where is Sal?'

'We'll see him soon. I can't always be with you, so I've asked Sal to look after you.' No sooner had she said this than Sal swam towards them.

Sal did the complete Royal flip in front of her, 'At your service, Princess Ally.'

'Don't do the flip for me.'

'But I have to. Unless you command me not to.'

'OK, I do. And just call me Ally.'

'Is that a command as well?' Sal's eyes twinkled with laughter.

'Yeah, it is.'

Alice told him about the attack on the way to the palace. 'I'll be escorting you from now on; it's too risky for Zina. Once we're through the forest, Fino will take you to the beach. You'll be safe. Now I will show you more of your kingdom. You haven't seen the park. Come on!' Sal held out his hand and pulled her off the shell she'd been sitting on.

The park was a meadow of ornamental seaweeds and grasses. Seahorses and brilliant red starfish floated gently past. Pink anemones and other peculiar looking things decorated the seabed. Alice didn't know what they were, 'Look at that one! It looks like a trumpet standing on end, and this one's like a bunch of tubes.'

'Wait till you see the coral reefs, we've a fantastic collection,' Sal said.

Alice saw many wonderful things she'd never seen before. Swimming from coral to coral she squealed with delight: one looked like broccoli, another like a head of lettuce, one a mushroom. 'It's like a vegetable garden.' She pointed at coral resembling celery, and another a bunch of grapes, 'Pity you can't eat them!'

'They are too beautiful to eat, even if we could. We eat specially grown kelp and algae instead.'

Alice loved what she was seeing and Sal's smiling face told her that it pleased him. 'Look here! This coral looks like a bunch of fingers with nail varnish on.' She pulled a face, 'Horrible! And here are some floating sea grass balls, what a luminous green colour!' Alice tossed one towards Sal. 'And this coral is like a yellow tree and this one a green grass fan.' She twirled several times; trying to take in the wonderful sights all at once.

Sal pointed out the keepers working in the park. They carried tools, which were shaped out of shells. 'We protect our garden. In your world, Ally, I know coral are lost because of pollution.' Sal shook his head, 'Your people let sewage and pesticides into the sea. So algae grow; blocking out the light. That's bad, Ally. Coral can't live without light. No coral, no fish. We need fish to eat the algae, otherwise it takes over.'

'Wicked!'

'Many humans know it's important to save the sea. We are getting some help now, but it's a struggle. Not enough of your people take it seriously.'

'My granny does. She says that huge nets are used; even catching fish they don't want, so they're thrown back dead. Small fish haven't got time to grow up. Hundreds of seabirds, turtles and dolphins are caught in the nets and die. I could cry, when I think about it.'

'Sounds like you have a smart Granny. I like her.' Sal smiled.

'Yeah, she's great.' Alice nodded. 'I'm proud of her. By the way, do you swim in the sea in our world?'

'We do, sometimes, but usually in groups; it's dangerous. We risk being eaten as we are so small. We use the camouflage cape, but it slows us down, can't see much with that on. Zina swims without it, that's how you found her.'

Alice nodded.

Sal continued, 'The king doesn't approve, and she should listen to her parents. They only think of her safety. But if she had, we wouldn't have met you.'

Zina swam up to them, 'Looks like you're having a good time.'

'He's great company,' Alice smiled.

'Sal will take you back now, but Father says you must take guards with you.'

Four stingrays formed a circle around Alice and Sal and escorted them to the Forest Gate where she waved goodbye.

Alice swam through the gate, where Fino would be waiting on the other side. She ran her hand under the scales to find the pocket. Where was it? She couldn't find it! She panicked. Sal and the guards had left, she had to stay calm. Without the berry she couldn't become human again. It would be too dangerous to swim back to the palace, she could be attacked.

What could she do? Of course, she remembered: the sea cape!

'Sea cape attach to me!' she shouted. At once a spotted blanket floated above her. With the camouflage cape shielding her from view, she was safe at least for the time being. Again she ran her fingers under the scales. Suddenly she became aware of a big eye looking at her, from under the side of the cape. It was Fino!

'Fino, talk to me! I can understand everything you say. The king gave me this power.' Alice didn't mean to shout, but she did.

'Great! But what are you doing, Ally?'

'I can't believe I'm talking to you! Somehow the noises you're making are translated for me. But I'm looking for the pocket with the berries. What if I can't find it?'

'Don't worry, Ally, I can send a message to Sal and he'll come back.'

'Good, I didn't think of that. Perhaps the pocket is further down? Yes, here it is!' She pulled out a berry and swallowed it. She remembered to hold the remaining berries, so that they would stay in her hand when she became human.

'I'm pleased the king gave you the magic to speak to me, I was hoping he would.' Fino took a big leap out of the sea and did a somersault in the air without touching the water. 'You're my heroine. You saved my friend Zina and the queen.' Then Fino got really excited, 'Watch this!' He set off gathering speed, and shot out of the water doing a triple somersault in front of her.

'Wicked,' Alice shouted, clapping her hands.

Fino surfaced by her side. 'You see, Zina once saved my life. I was caught in a fisherman's net, and she helped to free me.'

'Did she? Tell me how it happened.'

'Well, I thrashed about in this net trying to get loose and I only made it worse. Luckily for me Zina came along, she made me turn this way and that way, but it didn't work. She tried so hard it made her exhausted and then she went for help. Left alone, I was frightened. I didn't think I'd live. Would she come back? I couldn't be sure and nearly gave up.'

'But Zina came back. She'd never let anyone down,' Alice said.

'Yes, Zina returned with Sal and Link and many

of their men. Together they set me free. That was the first time I met Zina.'

'She's wonderful, we're lucky to have her as a friend.'

Fino nodded. 'Your friends are nice too. I've enjoyed playing with them. We did have fun! I wish we could do it again.'

'It's a shame we can't, but, Fino, at last I can ask you. Are you always on your own?'

'Oh no! I go back to my dolphin friends, when I'm not with you or Zina.'

'Good! I'd hate to think of you being on your own. I'd like you to meet my cat. His name is Simba.' Before she said goodbye to Fino, she told him all about Simba and her family.

Chapter 18

# Simba Goes to Sea

When she got back home, Alice had forgotten about being locked out but she found Simba waiting by the garden gate and he had a plan. 'I'll meow very loudly, until someone comes down and opens the door. They won't lock it again, so you can sneak in.'

'Good idea, Simba, I'll hide behind the bushes.'

And that's exactly what they did. Alice sneaked back to her room, where Simba was sitting outside the door. 'Come in. I've had an idea. I bet you've never talked to a dolphin before?'

'You know I haven't,' Simba answered.

'Do you want to meet Fino?'

'How can I? I hate water.'

'I'll take you out in the dinghy. Go on, don't be a spoil-sport!'

'I'm not sure.'

'But you're my friend. Please, please, say you'll come. I'm bursting to show you the magic I can do, and Fino will be waiting for us.'

Simba hesitated, 'What if I get wet?'

'If you keep your claws in, I'll make sure you don't.'

'OK, I must be mad. I'm doing this for you, against my better judgement. Promise I won't get wet.'

'Promise!'

\*

Early the next morning Alice and Simba left the house, sneaking out of the veranda door. Only this time Alice was careful not to lock it behind her.

'You'll have to sit still, Simba, I'll swim out and push the dinghy in front of me.' Simba protested when she lifted him in, and nearly dug a claw into her arm. 'Stop it! And keep your claws in, unless you want this dinghy to sink, remember it's made of rubber. You did agree to come.'

'I'm not sure anymore. I thought you'd be in here with me.'

'No, I prefer to swim.'

'Don't let go of this dinghy, Ally, or I'll never speak to you again.'

'Just keep still. I can see Fino, he's not far away.' Simba huddled down and didn't say a word until they reached Fino.

'Fino, meet Simba. I told you about him.'

Fino raised his head and looked into the dinghy. 'Hi,' he said.

'Nice to meet you, I'm sure. If only there wasn't so much water,' Simba answered.

'You don't know what you're missing. It's a beautiful world, plenty of freedom to move about.' Fino dived and came up on the other side of the dinghy.

'Thanks, but no thanks. I like a comfortable house. I don't have to chase about for my food, like you do.'

'Keeps me fit. What do you do all day?' Fino asked.

'Oh, sunbathe, eat, sleep, and chase an occasional mouse. Not to eat, you understand.' Simba hastily added, 'Just for exercise.'

'Don't think you chase enough of them,' Fino said.

'No need to get personal,' Simba answered but in good humour.

Alice listened to their conversation with a smile. Suddenly the tone of Simba's voice changed and he scurried close to the side, peering into the water, 'Ally, where are you? I can't see you.' His voice no longer had the lazy drawl, but was quite sharp.

'I'm here, Simba.'

'Where?'

'Here, look closer!'

'I don't believe it,' he croaked, and nearly fell overboard: Alice had changed into a Water Girl!

Fino on the other hand twittered in delight and did a backwards flip, so close to the dinghy that it rocked, and sent water gushing over Simba. Water!

'I told you, I can do magic! Didn't I?' Alice smiled unconcerned, although she knew this was his worst nightmare. Simba had his second shock in just as many minutes.

It took a while before Simba answered and, when he did, it wasn't without an effort. 'I wish you'd warned me, Ally. You are so small, I could swallow you. Here I am drifting about in the open sea, and I'm wet! Please, please, be normal again!' Simba crouched down on the bottom of the dinghy and covered his eyes with his paws.

This wasn't like Simba. He'd never appeared this undignified. 'Sorry, if I scared you. I'll take the other berry now.' Alice said hurriedly. Simba's eyes remained closed.

'You can look. I'm me again.' Alice was hanging onto the side.

Simba opened his eyes, 'Thank goodness! I've had enough excitement to last me for a month. Can we go back now?'

Fino popped up his head by Alice's side, 'Stay and play with me. I promise not to splash Simba anymore.'

'Can't, Fino, there'll be people on the beach soon.' Alice shook her head.

'It was nice meeting you, I think,' Simba said to Fino.

'And you, since you're a friend of Princess Ally.'

'She really is a princess then?'

'Sure is.' Fino beamed.

'Bye for now, Fino, ask Sal to meet me at the Forest Gate tomorrow,' Alice said.

Back on the beach Alice lifted Simba out of the dinghy. His fur clung to his body and water dripped from his ears. It made him look a lot slimmer but you could still see the roundness of his belly. Alice began to laugh. 'You look funny.'

'How dare you laugh? It's your fault; you promised I wouldn't get wet.' Simba tried hard to sound dignified. 'And you looked funny "ha, ha," in the water as well.'

Alice felt guilty and ashamed; she'd never seen Simba cross before. 'Sorry, it was an accident. Please, don't be angry! And I'm sorry you didn't like me being a Water Girl. But Fino is nice, don't you think?' Alice picked up a towel to dry Simba.

'He's OK. But this stuff with you shrinking and

growing scales, it's not natural.'

'Course not! It's magic! I'm very lucky I can do it.'

Simba shook his head, 'If you say so. But this is the first and last time I'll go near water.'

## Chapter 19

# Alice is in Danger

The next morning as Alice swam up to Fino, he didn't have his usual smiley face; his mouth drooped at the corners. 'What's up? Aren't you pleased to see me?'

'Yes and no. The truth is that the king doesn't want you to come. He thinks it's too dangerous. Only Zina persuaded him; the king can't say "no" to her.'

'Surely it's safe now?'

'Not sure. The Dark Sea People don't forget that quickly. The king has allowed you to come, but only to say goodbye.'

'Oh no, but I'm their princess, I'm allowed to come and go as I like.'

'Yes, but this is for your safety. Your safety,' Fino repeated.

'Well, we'll see.' Alice took the tiny berry out of her swimsuit pocket. Holding it very carefully between her fingers, afraid that it might be swept away, she quickly swallowed it. She felt a rush of excitement as she looked down at her body covered with sparkling blue scales.

She dived into the cool and clear water following Fino down and caught up with him by the dense forest wall. They swam along the side until she found the red algae and brown kelp, which Zina had taught her to recognize as the Forest Gate. 'Bye, Fino, I can't wait to see my friends,' she called out. She lent against the kelp and pushed hard with her shoulder; it gave way and opened up for her.

'Wait, don't enter the forest until you know that Sal has arrived with the guards,' Fino shouted back.

'I'll see you later. I expect he is waiting on the other side.'

Fino moved forward, to stop her, but she swam through the opening. By chance she glanced down at her ring and the hairs on her neck stood up; the stone was throbbing and pulsating with a brilliant red glow.

Danger! Danger!

If only she'd listened to Fino! 'Help!' She hissed, and moved backwards.

Too late!

She was surrounded. What are these hideous creatures? These ghastly Beings were of the same size and shape as the colourful Water People, but there the likeness stopped. My word, they are ugly and evil looking, she thought, as her head began to spin. Her breath was tight in her chest. This can't be true, please, let it not be true! She stared as one of the creatures moved towards her, his legs were black and his upper body a bony white with black protruding spiky scales. Gasping she tried to look away but she was hypnotized by the yellow flashing eyes in front of her face. The creatures tightened the circle around her. She must rub the ring to send for help! But her rigid arms wouldn't move and she couldn't bring her hand over to rest on the ring.

'Rub it!' she mumbled, barely able to speak, 'rub the ring.' Her hand jerked back to life and she pressed down on the stone. At the same moment the creature reached out with his bony arm and grabbed her. His white skull came close to her face and he grinned, showing off spiky teeth. She flinched at the sharp pain as his long nail pushed into the flesh of her arm. She tried to scream, but no sound came. In a haze she felt herself being lifted onto a frond, and tied up with a ribbon of thin sea-grass. She watched as the creatures lined up on either side, pulling the frond along with them.

This can't be happening, she thought, I am having a nightmare. I've been captured by the Dark Sea People!

The frond rocked uncomfortably as they carried her along. Apart from the Dark Sea People, she counted four conger eels and at least a dozen stingrays. The feared moustached fish swam towards her from a short distance away. He's their spy, she thought, and closed her eyes as his hairy moustache floated across her face. It was probably thanks to him, that she'd been captured. Where were they taking her? What a fool she'd been! If only she'd listened to the warnings. Now she'd put everyone in danger. With her as a hostage, the king would give in to the Dark Sea People's demand and give them the secret of the berries. Her effort to save the queen had been in vain. She hadn't deserved to become their princess.

The creatures looked straight ahead, only glancing at her now and then, with their yellow eyes flashing. Tears burnt her eyes; she was really, really scared. What if she never saw her family again?

Her family!

The thought of them made her strength return, and courage flooded through her. She wasn't going to give up without a fight. No way! I can beat them, she thought.

She pulled hard at the cords binding her, and

found that they loosened more easily than she had expected. She wriggled free. With energy surging through her, she made her body taut like the string on a bow, ready to shot off the arrow. And now she was the arrow! With a jolt she bounced off the frond, knocking over the Dark Sea Person next to her. The creatures were taken completely by surprise. It gave her enough time to get away before the Dark Sea People realized what was happening. Alice swam the fastest she'd ever swum in her life. Behind her she heard the stingrays and eels chasing after her, closing in, almost by her side now. 'I will escape. I must!' she muttered between gritted teeth.

Suddenly the eels and rays slowed down, Alice cheered when she realized the reason for this; in front of her was an advancing army of Water Men carrying spears! They were led by Sal and Link.

Sal swam up to her, 'Stay here Princess Ally, where you'll be safe. We'll fight them off.'

'No, Sal, I will not. This is my fight.'

'We can't allow you to fight, Princess Ally. We must keep you safe.'

'But if I command, you must do as I say.' Alice said.

Sal bowed his head, 'That's true, but …'

Alice interrupted, 'I command you.'

Sal looked into her eyes and only hesitated for a moment, 'You need a weapon, here take my spear. I will use my dagger.'

She reached out to receive the spear, 'Now, we'll fight them off together.'

The Water People had already attacked and fought bravely but the congers gave the Dark Sea People the upper hand. The eels swam with a terrific speed, from one Water Man to the next, hitting them hard with their tails. This wasn't going well! A forceful whack on the legs sent her rescuers down to the sea bed, unable to swim. Once there it took them some time to recover from the blow.

But now the Dark Sea People seemed confused and were hesitating. Alice sensed that the mood had changed and when a huge eel appeared out of the seaweed, she knew why. The eel had enormous teeth, and she recognized him as a moray eel. Great! He is chasing off the congers, he's on our side. The Water People cheered when they saw the moray eel and moved faster. Their spears swished through the water sending the enemy to the sea bed.

'Look out, Sal!' Alice shouted, as a stingray came at full speed attacking from behind. But Link had also seen that his brother was in danger and, quick as lightning, he speared the ray before it reached Sal. Alice sighed with relief as Sal turned and sped towards her with a reassuring smile, the next second he was by her side.

Together they swam into the thick of the battle.

Alice caught sight of the Dark Sea Person, who had punctured her arm. With a flick of her flipper feet she surged towards him and gripping her spear with both hands; she whacked his legs with all her might. He sank to the sea bed, joining the others who had lost their fight.

Alice turned around searching for the nearest enemy. To her horror she saw that a Dark Sea Person had extended his index finger into a long sharp weapon, and intended to strike Link in his back.

'Link!' She yelled and lunged forward, bringing down her spear on the attacker's legs. Link turned around in time to see her blow miss the target. The Dark Sea Person furiously advanced on Alice instead. Now Link came to the rescue, he struck out with one swift blow and she watched her attacker sink to the bottom.

The battle had been won. The defeated Dark Sea Beings retreated. The Water People gathered together their injured fighters from the sea bed. Those who hadn't recovered; formed a chain and were towed back to the palace. A friendly octopus helped them over the palace wall by carrying several of them at the time, one on each of his tentacles.

Waiting by the palace entrance were Zina, the king and queen. Sal and Link told them about the fight and Alice's part in it.

'She was fantastic!' Sal shot a glance at Alice.

'Yeah, she sure knows how to fight.' Link added.

Zina's cheeks got red. 'You mean to say that she joined in the fight?'

'She did! And saved me from a nasty injury,' Link said.

'If only I had been there,' Zina said wistfully, 'but father won't let me fight.'

'You know only too well, why not,' the queen said.

Zina hung her head, 'Yes, Mother, but it's not fair.'

Sal turned to Alice, 'Sorry, we weren't at the Forest Gate to meet you. The Dark Sea People stopped us from getting there, by attacking us on the way. I got the signal from the ring; that you were in danger. But we had to fight off the first lot before we could get to you.' Sal explained.

'Straight into another fight,' Alice said.

Zina linked arms with Alice, 'Their spies told the Dark Sea People that you were coming. The message we sent to Fino; asking him to meet you, was intercepted. We've changed the frequency now. The Dark Sea People came to capture you. We don't often see them.'

'I thought I was going to die,' Alice said.

The king's frown deepened, 'No, they wanted you alive.' The king paused, his eyes sad, 'Princess Ally, let this be a lesson to you.'

'I'm sorry, Your Majesty, I should've listened to you. I promise I will, if only I can come back. Please!' She had let the king down and yet he wasn't angry with her, just sad. It made her regret her action even more.

'Don't be sorry, Princess Ally! With your help we have defeated the Dark Sea People and our secret of the berry is safe. You can come, but the water is turning cold now, we must wait for it to grow warm again. The moon will have to pass many times.' The king's face lit up, 'And Zina will visit you on land. You see, she's been granted her Land Adventure Expedition.'

'Oh, Zina, I can't wait,' Alice hugged her friend. 'I will show you many things. It'll be so exciting!'

Zina did a backward flip. 'I'll be able to meet your family. And I can tell them about saving the sea.'

The queen interrupted, 'Sorry, girls, but Alice must leave. Considering what's happened; we must cut her visit short.'

She left the palace with Sal and guards, Zina and her parents came as far as the palace gate. Alice swam for a short distance and then stopped.

'Wait, Sal!' Blinking away a tear she turned and waved to her friends. But she knew that she wanted to go home to her mum and dad. And Joseph, she missed him too, and Simba.

'I'm not crying, and I'm not sad. I'm happy,' she laughed. 'Sal, let's hurry!'

As she swam away she could hear Zina call out, 'See you next year, Ally!'

The End

COMING SOON

# Alice and Friends in her Secret World

Sequel to The Water People's Secret

# Chapter One
## Many Moons have Passed

*Dear Diary,*

*Today the most amazing thing in the world has happened to me. I've made friends with a girl from another world. It's true! I went for a walk on the beach and there she was, trapped in a shell! She is really tiny, but very pretty with the most amazing copper red hair and her body is covered in sparkling green scales. Her name is Princess Zina. She comes from the Water People's world hidden beneath the waves. Isn't it great!*

Alice shifted her weight, she'd found the only sandy spot on the pebbled beach to sit on. She'd brought her diary with her to read and before she put it back in her bag, she checked the date of the entry, which she'd made the previous year, 21 April. So much had happened since that first meeting. With the use of the magic berry she'd been able to visit Zina's under water world, where many exciting things had taken place.

A year had passed and she hoped that the adventures would start all over again. She shielded her eyes from the sun and looked out to sea for Fino, a dolphin friend of the Water People and, now also her friend. Zina's father, the king, had given her the power to talk to all sea creatures. Fino would tell her when she could go back to Zina's world. She stood up and scanned the horizon for his fin. Where was he? But there was no sign of him. Guess I'll have to wait another day, a heavy sigh escaped her.

Her eyes wandered along the beach. It was warm in the water for the end of June and a few people were swimming. Her older brother Joseph and his friend Tom paddled with their jeans-legs pulled up, splashing water on each other and getting soaked. Alice shook her head, they are behaving like five year olds, she thought. Although she liked Tom, she wished that he hadn't let his blond hair grow quite so long, and not to mention the ear ring. He had to remove it for school, but still. Why did he wear it? But he was always helpful and smiley. Both boys were tall and slim, Tom being the shorter of the two. Joseph is as tall as Mum now, she thought, as he put his hand up and waved to her.

The sea was calm and as she took a deep breath of the sea air, she caught a whiff of rotting seaweed. She grimaced, the smell was horrid.

'Ouch!' She turned sharply as a ball hit her in the back, showering her with sand. 'Look out, where you throw that,' she said to the boy, who came running after it.

'Sorry!' The boy reached out for the ball.

Alice stood up and brushed off the sand. At first she only glanced at the tall girl coming out of the water. But her head jerked back again. There was no mistaking that red hair! No one else had hair like that. Alice called out but only managed a croaking noise. Her legs turned into spaghetti and she sat back on the sand with a thump. But the girl with the copper red hair and the sparkling emerald green costume knew exactly where she was going. She headed straight for her, and she was in a hurry.

'Hi, Ally!'

'Zina!' Alice jumped up, throwing her arms around her friend, her head spinning. 'Zina,' she repeated, 'I can't believe it's you. You look so human!' She pulled away, 'But ouch, you're cold!'

'It's me all right,' Zina laughed. 'Well, yes, you know I'm fish. My blood isn't warm like yours.'

'I forgot, it was a bit of a shock. But I've been waiting for Fino and here you are. I've missed you!'

'Me too! It's many moons since I saw you.'

'I'm so excited…' But Alice's smile died away as Zina frowned and grabbed her arm.

'Ally, you've got to help. There's no time to lose...

Made in the USA
Charleston, SC
28 May 2014